Wonder Kid Meets the Evil Lunch Snatcher

Wonder Kid Meets the Evil Lunch Snatcher

by Lois Duncan

Illustrated by Margaret Sanfilippo

Little, Brown and Company

Boston   Toronto

07

For Erin and Brittany Mahrer
with love

Text Copyright © 1988 by Lois Duncan
Illustrations Copyright © 1988 by Little, Brown
and Company (Inc.)

First Edition

Library of Congress Cataloging-in-Publication Data
Duncan, Lois, 1934–
    Wonder Kid meets the evil lunch snatcher / by Lois Duncan.
    p.   cm. — (A Springboard book)
    Summary: Terrorized by an evil lunch-snatcher at his new school,
Brian devises, with the help of a fellow comic book fan, a plan
involving a new superhero called Wonder Kid.
    ISBN 0-316-19558-8
    [1. Bullies — Fiction.   2. Moving, Household — Fiction.
3. Schools — Fiction.]   I. Title.
PZ7.D9117WO   1988
[E] — dc19
                                                    87-26490
                                                        CIP
                                                        AC

10 9 8 7 6 5 4 3 2 1

WOR

Published simultaneously in Canada
by Little, Brown & Company (Canada) Limited

Printed in the United States of America

1

Right from the start Brian Johnson had known it would be a bad day.

Actually, it had been a bad month and a bad year. His father had lost his job and been offered another in a faraway town, so the Johnson family had been forced to move in the middle of the school year.

This particular day, though, started out wrong at breakfast. Brian was late to the table, and by the time he got there, his father was getting ready to go off to work, and his seven-year-old sister, Sarah, was cramming down the last of the sweet rolls. There was nothing left but cereal and cold toast.

Their mother was standing at the counter, making lunches.

"What on earth have you been doing so long?" she asked Brian.

"He was reading in the bathroom," said Sarah in a tattle-tale voice. "I know, because when I went in to brush my teeth I found one of his comic books on the floor."

"I don't know why you read that junk, Brian," their father said as he opened the door to leave. "With so many good books around, why do you waste your time on comics?"

"I don't know," Brian said. "I just sort of like them."

Actually, he *did* know why he liked to read old-time comic books. When a guy was shy and skinny, it was comforting to imagine what it would be like to be a powerful superhero like Spiderman or Captain Marvel or Superman.

"You picked a bad time to get caught up in reading," his mother said. "Hurry up now and eat. You don't want to be late for your first day at your new school."

Brian sat down at the table in front of his bowl of cereal. Then he poured in milk. He ate a few bites and pushed the bowl away.

"I'm not very hungry," he said.

His mother set the lunches on the table.

"I know it's hard to eat when you're excited," she said.

"*I'm* excited, and *I* ate *my* breakfast," bragged Sarah. Sarah was always happy to gobble up anything.

"You and your brother are two different people," said their mother. She ruffled

Brian's hair in a loving way. "If you're sure you're finished, you and Sarah had better get going."

Brian slid out from under her hand and got up from the table.

He picked up his lunch sack. It was heavy. His mother always made good lunches.

His mother bent and kissed him. Then she kissed Sarah, leaving a red smudge on her cheek. Brian quickly wiped off his own cheek. The last thing he needed was to start his first day at Summerfield School smeared with lip-stick.

"Have a happy day, kids," their mother said. "I know it's a little bit scary starting school in a new town, but think of all the wonderful friends you will make here! I'm sure in no time at all you will be having just as much fun at this new school as you did at your old one."

Her words kept ringing in Brian's ears after he and Sarah left the house. They made him feel sad and guilty. Just because he made the honor roll and his teachers said nice things about him, his parents thought he was well-adjusted and popular.

How disappointed they would be if they ever guessed the truth — that their son was a nerd.

Brian knew he would not make friends in Summerfield. He knew this because he hadn't had friends at his old school. The only people there who had even bothered to talk to him were a few wimpy kids who were nearly as nerdy as he was.

Summerfield School was only three blocks from the Johnson's new house. As he and Sarah walked toward it, Brian felt his stomach churning. He was glad his mother had not made him finish his breakfast.

The lower end of the school grounds was cut off from the street by a high hedge. Over the tips of the bushes, Brian could see the top of a swing set and the upper bars of a jungle gym.

There was a gateway cut in the hedge so people could walk through.

On the other side of the hedge a bell started ringing.

"We're late!" cried Sarah. "Oh, Brian, you made us late! You and your dumb old comics made us late our very first day!"

"I don't think we're *that* late," Brian said hopefully. "That's just the first bell. We'll still get to class on time."

"Well, hurry up!" snapped Sarah. "You're slow as a snail!"

She left his side and broke into a run.

Even though she was pudgy, his sister ran surprisingly fast. She went zipping through the opening in the hedge like a plump little bunny plunging into a rabbit hole.

"I told you, we're not going to be late!" Brian called after her. Then, beginning to feel worried, he too started to run.

He had almost reached the hole in the hedge when he heard Sarah scream.

"That's mine!" she shrieked. "You can't have that! Give it back!"

2

Brian raced through the opening in the hedge and burst out onto the playground.

What he saw there stopped him dead in his tracks.

Sarah was surrounded by a group of five tough-looking boys.

The largest of them had thick, black hair that stood up on his head in spikes. In his hand he was holding a brown paper sack.

"What are you doing with my sister's

lunch?" cried Brian. He wanted his voice to sound threatening, but it squeaked in a funny way.

"This isn't your sister's lunch anymore," said the boy. He opened the sack and began to rummage inside it. "Hey, look what a lot of stuff she has in here! Five chocolate chip cookies! That's one for each of us."

He took a bite of one cookie and tossed the others to his friends.

They all popped them into their mouths and started chewing.

"You robbers!" Sarah exploded. "Those cookies are mine!"

"I always like to eat dessert first," said the boy. "Now let's see what you've brought for my main course." He reached into the sack again and pulled more things out. "An apple, chips, and a sandwich. I wonder what kind it is." He unwrapped the sandwich and held it up to his nose. "Yuck! It smells like tuna. I can't stand tuna."

He dropped the sandwich onto the ground and put his foot on it.

The tuna filling squished out on both sides of his shoe.

Brian stared at the boy in disbelief.

"You can't do that!" he exclaimed. "You're wrecking her lunch!"

"That's a punishment for breaking the rules," said the boy.

12

"What rules?" cried Sarah. "I didn't do anything wrong!"

"You came through the Sixth-Grade Gate," the boy told her. "Only big kids are allowed to come in this entrance."

"I didn't know that," said Sarah. "The hedge didn't have a sign on it. Besides, that doesn't mean you can eat my cookies!"

The other four boys burst out laughing.

"You must be new here," one of them said. "Nobody tells Matt Gordon what he can't do. If Matt wants to eat cookies, Matt eats cookies."

"I'm going to tell!" Sarah shouted.

"No, you won't," said the boy named Matt. "Any kid who snitches on me is asking for trouble." He turned to Brian. "You came through the Sixth-Grade Gate too. That means I get two lunches instead of one."

"Don't you come near me!" said Brian, backing away.

"I'll do whatever I want!" Matt Gordon told him.

He lunged for Brian and grabbed the lunch sack out of his hand.

"Now, get out of here!" he commanded. "Be quick about it, too, or I'll step on your face just the way I stepped on that sandwich."

"Come on, Sarah," said Brian, grabbing his sister's hand.

He backed through the hole in the hedge, dragging Sarah with him.

I ought to be standing up to that creep, he thought miserably. The kids at my old school were right then they called me a wimp!

"So the lunch-snatcher gang got two new victims!" a voice said.

Brian spun around to find a boy watching him from the sidewalk. The boy had curly red hair and was wearing glasses.

"The other day I forgot and went in through that gate," he said. "Matt and his gang pulled my lunch apart and stamped on it."

"Why didn't you tell your teacher?" asked Sarah, blinking back tears. Sarah always hated to cry in front of strangers.

"Nobody snitches on Matt," the boy said bitterly. "Last year he picked on a first-grader, and she told her dad. He went to the principal, and Matt got detention. After that, he and his friends made that poor kid's life so miserable her folks had to put her in a private school."

Brian was so shocked he could hardly speak. "Can't *anybody* do *anything?* That guy's a *criminal!*"

The boy shook his head. "Matt runs the school. It would take a superhero to bring him to justice."

"It would take a . . . *what?*" Brian couldn't believe what he'd heard.

"A superhero," the boy repeated. "You know — like Batman. Or Plastic Man or Wonder Woman or — "

He broke off suddenly as though he were

afraid Brian would make fun of him.

"Or Captain Marvel," said Brian. "Or Spiderman or Superman."

The red-haired boy stared at him in astonishment.

"Do you read comic books too?"

"I have a whole collection," said Brian. "My dad calls them junk, but I feel good when I read them."

"I know. They make you feel powerful," the boy said, nodding. "My name's Robbie Chandler. I'm in fourth grade."

"I'm Brian Johnson," said Brian. "I'm in fourth grade too."

From behind the hedge, there came the sound of the bell again.

"That's the second bell!" shrieked Sarah. "Now we're *really* late!"

"We're late," agreed Robbie. "But we're all of us late together."

All of a sudden Brian found himself feeling much better.

16

3

The fourth-grade classroom at Summerfield School was not much different from the fourth-grade classroom back at Brian's old school. The desks were arranged the same way, and the big hand on the wall clock jumped from minute to minute with the same sharp clicking sound as the clock on the wall of his old classroom.

The two rooms even smelled the same, like chewing gum and tennis shoes and chalk dust.

And peanut butter.

And chocolate cake.

And bananas.

As the morning passed and the sack lunches that were stored in the cubbies at the back of the classroom got warmer and riper, Brian became more and more hungry. By the time twelve o'clock rolled around, his stomach was growling so loudly it sounded like a caged tiger.

"Whenever you children are finished eating you can go out and play," said their teacher, Mrs. Busby.

Brian felt sure he was going to like Mrs. Busby. She had kind eyes and a voice with a smile in it, and even though it was only his first day at Summerfield, she already knew his name.

"Didn't you bring a lunch, Brian?" she asked him.

For a moment Brian considered telling her what had happened to his lunch. Then he remembered Matt Gordon's words: "Any kid who snitches on me is asking for trouble."

There was no way he wanted trouble from Matt and his buddies.

"I did bring a lunch," he said. "I'm just not hungry."

Since he had nothing to eat, he got up and went outside. The playground was crowded with children. He glanced about him, feeling left out and lonely, the way he had often felt back at his old school.

At least he did not see Matt Gordon and his friends. Sixth-graders must have a later recess, he thought.

Suddenly he caught sight of his sister sitting on a bench. She was jabbering away at a girl with bright red hair.

Brian walked over to where the two girls were sitting. When he reached them he saw that they were eating potato chips.

"Hi," said Sarah. "This is Lisa, Robbie Chandler's sister. She's in third grade, and she's sharing her lunch with me. Lisa, this is my brother, Brian."

"Sarah told me what happened this morning," said Lisa. "I know what it's like to be jumped by Matt and his gang. On my birthday my mother baked cupcakes for all the kids in my class. The minute I came through the gate, Matt grabbed the box away."

"Hey, Brian!" Robbie's voice rang out across the playground.

Brian turned and saw his new friend hurrying toward them.

"You took off so fast, I couldn't catch up with you," Robbie said. He thrust a half of a sandwich into Brian's hand. "I hope you like cheese and tomato. That's all my mom packed today."

"Gee, thanks," said Brian, who would happily have eaten *anything*. He wolfed down

the sandwich so quickly he didn't even taste it.

"We were talking about that awful Matt," said Sarah. "I wish somebody would teach that bully a lesson."

"Like a superhero, maybe?" Robbie said, laughing. "It's too bad those powerful guys aren't real."

"Nobody has ever *proved* they aren't real," said Brian.

"Oh, come on!" exclaimed Sarah. "You know they're made up!"

"But what if they weren't?" said Brian. "Who would ever know it? Superheroes go around disguised as ordinary people. It's only when they're fighting evil that they put on their masks and costumes and start flying and jumping over buildings and zapping criminals."

"Sometimes they don't even have to zap criminals," said Robbie. "Sometimes the bad guys just get so scared they surrender."

Brian said, "I bet Matt would think twice about robbing people if he thought a super-hero was out to get him."

"He would never believe that," said Sarah.

"Most people believe what they read in the paper," said Lisa. She seemed to be thinking hard as she munched her potato chips. "It's possible Matt might believe a newspaper story, especially if there was a picture that went along with it."

"How could we get a story like that in the paper?" asked Sarah.

"Lisa could do it!" said Robbie. "She's a reporter for our school paper. She's always writing stories about interesting people."

"But the picture?" said Sarah. "Who would pose for that?"

"I would!" Brian said excitedly. "I could dress up in that Superman costume I wore on Halloween! Nobody could tell who it was if I wore a mask!"

"I wore a Spiderman costume last Halloween," said Robbie. "We could use the hood from that to cover up your hair."

Sarah regarded the two boys doubtfully. "Aren't superheros big?"

"Not when they're young," said Brian. "Everybody starts out as a kid."

"I'd need help writing the story," Lisa told them. "I don't know much about how superheroes do things."

"No problem!" Robbie said with a grin. "Brian and I are experts! We'll come up with a story that will knock Matt Gordon's socks off!"

4

The paper with Lisa's article came out the next Monday.

By noon, the issue had sold out.

By the following day, even students who had not purchased the paper had read the copies their friends had bought, and everybody was talking about the superhero story.

Sarah felt very proud because she was in

it. She kept the article in her desk and read it over and over:

Sarah Johnson is a new second-grade student at Summerfield School. She says she likes it at Summerfield, but she misses her good friend Wonder Kid, who was a classmate at her old school.

"Wonder Kid is a superhero," says Sarah. "He rights wrongs. He protects the innocent. He leaps tall buildings with a single bound. He zaps criminals, especially lunch snatchers."

Sarah says Wonder Kid often flies here to visit her.

"Once a friend, always a friend," says Sarah.

Next to the story there was a snapshot of a boy wearing a cape and a mask. On the front of his shirt was a big letter W. The boy's arms were bulging with muscles.

26

He was pointing a finger at the camera.

The caption under the picture read: "*Criminals better shape up! Wonder Kid zaps!*"

By the end of the third day, Sarah had read the story so many times she was even beginning to imagine it was true.

"Look how strong Wonder Kid's arms are!" she said.

"Are you nuts?" Brian snorted. "You were there when we made those muscles. They're nothing but Mother's panty hose all bunched up."

"I know," Sarah sighed, "but they really do look awesome."

She was starting to like the thought of having a friend like Wonder Kid.

A lot of people seemed to believe the story, especially kids who watched a lot of television.

There were others, however, who did not take it seriously. Lisa's teacher complimented her on writing "such a cute little piece of fiction," and the kids in her enriched science class thought it was a joke.

"The only thing that counts is what Matt

thinks," said Robbie. "We can't blow our scheme by asking him, so we'll have to run a test."

"What sort of test?" asked Brian.

"Sarah will have to go through the Sixth-Grade Gate again," said Robbie. "If Matt and his gang don't jump her, we'll know they're scared."

Sarah did not like that idea one bit.

"It's not fair!" she said. "I don't want my lunch to be snatched again!"

"Let's take a vote," said Brian. "All in favor of running this test, raise your hand . . . "

The vote came out three to one in favor of the test.

Unable to argue further, Sarah gave in.

When she walked through the hole in the hedge, Matt was right there waiting.

"Look who's here!" he crowed. "The lunch-delivery girl!" With one quick grab, he had Sarah's sack in his hand.

"You give that back, or I'm going to call Wonder Kid!" Sarah shrieked.

"I don't believe that stupid story," Matt told her. "If Wonder Kid is your buddy, where are you keeping him?"

Sarah did not stop to think before she spoke.

"You'll see him tomorrow!" she cried. "He's coming to visit! I've told him about how you lunch snatchers pick on people. He's coming to take revenge and protect his friends!"

"That's a crock of lies," said Matt, but he sounded uncertain.

He tossed Sarah's lunch sack back to the boy behind him.

"You can have this," he said. "It's probably tuna sandwiches."

"I don't want it," his friend said quickly. "I ate a big breakfast."

"I won't believe in this superdude till I've seen him," Matt told Sarah. "Bring him here to meet me tomorrow morning."

Sarah suddenly realized she had gone too far.

"He can't come tomorrow," she said. "Tomorrow's a school day."

"Wonder Kid goes to school!" Matt exclaimed in amazement. "Why would a superhero waste time in a classroom?"

"He doesn't think it's a waste of time," said Sarah. "Wonder Kid believes in education." She tried to remember the exact words her brother had used earlier. "Superheroes spend most of their time disguised as ordinary people. Wonder Kid goes to school like any other kid."

"Okay," said Matt. "You can bring him here after school then. But tell him he'd better be ready to show off his zapping."

5

"How could you have agreed to such a thing!" Brian exploded.

"I didn't know how to get out of it," said Sarah.

"So, what's the problem?" asked Robbie. "Why *can't* Matt meet Wonder Kid? All Brian has to do is put on his superhero costume."

"Matt doesn't want to *meet* Wonder Kid," said Brian. "What he wants is to see Wonder Kid in action."

"Then Wonder Kid can zap somebody," said Robbie. "That shouldn't be too hard to arrange. My grandfather gave me a magic set last Christmas. The wand has a battery in it that shoots off sparks."

"And we've got smoke bombs left over from Fourth of July," Lisa reminded him. "Remember how it rained so we couldn't shoot them off? Wonder Kid can appear in a cloud of smoke!"

Everybody was getting excited except Brian.

"If I zap Matt, and he doesn't feel it, he'll know Wonder Kid's a fake," he said.

"Then don't zap Matt," said Robbie. "Zap somebody else."

"Let's take a vote like we did before," suggested Sarah. "Everybody in favor of having Matt meet Wonder Kid, raise your hand."

The vote came out three to one in favor of the meeting.

Brian's stomach lurched in exactly the way

it had on his first day at the new school. Maybe he was getting the flu, he told himself hopefully.

The next morning he did wake up feeling sick, but not sick enough.

"You don't have a temp," said his mother, feeling his forehead. "I think it will be all right for you to go to school today."

Robbie had worked out the plan the evening before. Brian was to take his superhero costume and raincoat to school in his bookbag. He would store the bag in his cubby, and as soon as school let out, he would take it into the boys' room and change into Wonder Kid.

Then he would put his raincoat on over his costume.

Brian felt more and more nervous as the day went on. No matter how hard he tried, he could not keep his mind on his schoolwork.

34

Mrs. Busby had to call his name three times when it was his turn to do the times tables, and even then he couldn't remember the sixes.

Mrs. Busby looked worried.

"Brian, are you feeling all right?" she asked. "You got every one of your number facts right on yesterday's quiz. I can't believe you've forgotten the sixes already."

"I'm fine," said Brian, and wished that it were not true. He would have been much happier if he had been sent to the nurse's office.

The minute hand on the wall clock kept zipping along so fast that the day seemed to pass like a shot. When it made its final click into place and the bell rang to signal that school was out, Brian knew the moment he had been dreading had come at last.

He got up from his desk and walked slowly back to his cubby.

Robbie clapped him on the shoulder as he went by.

"Don't look so worried," he said. "We can pull it off."

"What do you mean, 'we'?" Brian snapped. "*I'm* the one who has to go out there with that dumb costume on."

"Stop making such a big deal out of this," said Robbie. "You seemed to like the costume when you wore it for the picture."

"Well, I don't like it now," said Brian. "This is a dumb idea."

Brian got his bookbag out of his cubby and took it with him into the boys' room. To his relief, nobody else was in there.

He went into one of the stalls and changed into all of the costume except the Spider-man hood. The big yellow *W* that Lisa had sewed onto the Superman shirt was beginning to come loose, so he stuck it back down with a glue stick he'd borrowed from art class.

Then he took his mother's panty hose out of the bookbag and wadded it up and stuffed

36

it into his shirt. The bunched-up hose had looked like muscles in the photograph. He hoped it would still look that way on the playground.

When Brian left the rest room, the janitor was standing out in the hall, emptying waste-paper baskets into a trash cart.

He looked surprised when he saw Brian in his raincoat.

"You must know something I don't," he said. "Last time I looked out the window, the sun was shining."

"You never can tell when it might start raining," said Brian. "Storms can come up pretty fast this time of year."

He walked down the hall and out of the school building. Sarah was waiting outside the door with a grocery sack. In the sack there were smoke bombs, a box of matches, and a long black wand.

"Where are Robbie and Lisa?" Brian asked his sister.

"Out on the playground behind the school," said Sarah.

She looked as excited as if she were going to a party.

"Let's hurry!" she squealed. "I can't wait to see Matt's face when he finally gets his chance to see Wonder Kid in action!"

6

Sarah continued to chatter like a happy little parrot as they walked along the sidewalk at the end of the school grounds.

Brian was too nervous to listen to her. He kept glancing at the hedge that cut off their view of the playground and wondering if Matt and his gang were behind it.

They stopped just short of the Sixth-Grade Gate so Brian could change the rest of the way into Wonder Kid.

He took the Spiderman hood out of his

bookbag and pulled it on over his head. Then he took off his raincoat.

A car passed by, and the driver turned around to stare at him. He looked as though he couldn't believe what he was seeing.

Brian's stomach did a flip-flop.

"I think I'm going to throw up," he said.

"Superheroes never throw up," said Sarah.

She opened the grocery sack and took out Robbie's wand. Brian took it from her and shoved it up his sleeve.

"Maybe Matt and his friends have forgotten to come," he said.

"I bet they haven't," said Sarah. "I'll check and see."

She dashed through the hole in the hedge and out onto the playground.

"They're here, all right!" she shouted back over her shoulder.

"Of course, we're here." Matt's voice sounded meaner than ever. "I see you're all by yourself. Where is your superbuddy?"

"He's coming," said Sarah. "He'll be along any minute now."

More than anything in the world, Brian wanted to run. Their house was only a couple of blocks away. In minutes he could be safely home with the door locked.

But that would mean leaving his sister alone with the lunch snatchers. He knew there was no way he could do that to Sarah.

He took the matches and a smoke bomb out of the grocery sack. He could not bend his right arm because of the wand, so he had to strike the match with his arms straight in front of him.

The matchstick snapped in two.

"Wonder Kid will be along any minute now," Sarah repeated loudly.

She paused a moment, and then she said it a third time.

Frantically, Brian yanked out another match

and struck it. This time the stick did not break, and the match burst into flame. With a gasp of relief, Brian held the flame to the wick of the smoke bomb. The bomb started to fizzle.

"This is it," Brian whispered. There was no turning back now. Crazy as the scheme might be, he had to go through with it.

Since he couldn't pitch with his stiff right arm, he took the bomb in his left hand and awkwardly tossed it in through the hole in the hedge. Then, before he could panic, he stepped through after it.

Thick, black smoke came billowing up all around him. He felt as though he were popping out through a cloud.

He heard a series of gasps from Matt and his friends.

All of a sudden, Brian didn't feel like a nerd anymore.

He felt like a guy who was able to leap tall buildings!

He felt like a hero who could bring evil criminals to justice!

"Do not fear! Wonder Kid's here!" he shouted. His voice rang out as powerful and strong as a superhero's.

"Here he is!" cried Sarah. "I knew my friend wouldn't fail me!"

Matt's buddies, who had been grouped around him, backed hastily away.

"I've got to get going," one said. "I've got homework to do."

"So do I," said another. "I have to study for a math quiz."

"Hey, what's with you guys?" exclaimed Matt. "Can't you see this guy's a fake? He doesn't have magic powers, and he isn't any superhero."

"He is, and he'll prove it!" cried Sarah. "Just wait till he zaps you!"

"He doesn't have to zap *me*," Matt said a bit nervously. "If he wants to zap somebody else, though, I don't mind watching."

"I really do need to go home now," said one of his friends.

"Don't be a coward," said Matt. "Stick around for the show."

"I never zap innocent people," Brian told them. "I'll prove my powers by zapping the roof off the school."

He raised his right arm and pointed his finger at the school. With his thumb, he pressed the switch on the wand from Robbie's magic set. The wand burst forth with a rattle like a machine gun, and a shower of sparks came shooting out of its tip.

The school did not seem to be injured, but a red-haired boy on the steps let out a terrible shriek and fell to the ground.

The girl who was standing next to him screamed in terror.

"My brother's been zapped!" Lisa cried. "Somebody call an ambulance!"

"I aimed too low," said Brian. "I'll try it again."

Once more he raised his arm and pointed his finger.

This time there was no one but Sarah to see what happened. Matt and his friends were halfway across the school yard.

7

The next issue of the school paper carried a banner headline: "SUMMERFIELD STUDENT ZAPPED BY SUPERHERO." The article read:

Robbie Chandler, a fourth-grade student at Summerfield School, was zapped on the playground last Tuesday.

The zapper was the well-known superhero Wonder Kid.

Sarah Johnson, who witnessed the

zapping, said it was an accident.

"Wonder Kid did not mean to zap Robbie," she said. "Smoke got in his eyes, and his aim was off."

Matt Gordon and his gang were witnesses too, but they got scared and ran away.

Next to the article there was a picture of Robbie with a bandage around his head. The caption said, *"Victim of tragic zapping accident."*

The paper sold out so fast a second edition had to be printed. Lisa was excused from class to help run the copy machine.

When school let out, Sarah found Matt Gordon and his gang waiting for her in the hall outside the second-grade classroom.

"Why did you tell that reporter we're scared of Wonder Kid?" Matt demanded. He looked and sounded furious.

"Because you are," said Sarah, trying not

to seem frightened. "As soon as you saw him zap Robbie, you turned and ran."

"I didn't run because I was scared," said Matt. "I ran because I thought I heard my mother calling. My friends and I think this Wonder Kid dude is a fake. We want to see him leap a tall building with a single bound."

"He's not free this afternoon," said Sarah. "He has to go to the dentist."

"Then he'd better be here first thing in the morning," Matt told her. "If we don't see Wonder Kid leap over a building, his 'good friend Sarah' won't be eating lunch for a year."

He screwed up his face into a horrible monster snarl. Behind him, all his gang members did the same thing. Sarah had never imagined they could look so awful.

"Oh, dear! I think I forgot my homework!" she said.

She rushed back into the classroom and slammed the door. It was ten whole minutes before she felt brave enough to open it again.

Finally she pulled it open just a crack and peeked out.

Matt and his friends were gone.

Sarah raced out of the room and down the hall. She zipped out of the building and ran at top speed all the way home.

Brian, Robbie, and Lisa were gathered in the Johnsons' front yard. They all had copies of the school paper and were taking turns reading Lisa's article out loud. They turned in surprise when Sarah came panting up to them.

"Where were you?" Lisa asked her. "I thought we were going to walk home from school together."

"Matt and his gang stopped me in the hall," explained Sarah. "Tomorrow morning they want to see Wonder Kid leap a building."

"There's no way Wonder Kid is going to do that," said Brian.

"But he has to!" cried Sarah. "If he doesn't, Matt will take away all my lunches for a year!"

Just thinking about it made her stomach growl with hunger.

"You know Wonder Kid can't jump over a building," said Brian. "You can't have forgotten his muscles are only panty hose."

There was a moment of silence.

Then Robbie said thoughtfully, "It's true that Wonder Kid can't jump over a building, but he might be able to make it over a hedge."

"That hedge by the playground? You've got to be kidding!" said Brian.

"We could set up a ladder behind the hedge," said Robbie. "If Wonder Kid jumped off that, he would land in the playground."

"Dad's stepladder is stored in our garage," said Lisa. "We could set that up on the sidewalk outside the Sixth-Grade Gate."

"I don't want to jump off a ladder," Brian said definitely.

"Let's vote," said Sarah. "Everybody in favor, raise your hand!"

Three hands shot up. Brian's hands went into his pockets.

"I won't do it," he said. "I won't jump off a ladder."

"Just think what a marvelous story it will make!" exclaimed Lisa. "I'm going to rush home right now and put film in the camera."

Brian said, "If I jump off a ladder, I'll break my legs."

"No, you won't," said Robbie. "We'll dig up the ground on the other side of the hedge. That way Wonder Kid will have a soft spot to land." He smiled his bright, sunny smile. He didn't seem worried at all.

"We'll hold a rehearsal first thing in the morning," he said.

8

The rehearsal was set for seven o'clock the next morning.

Brian had a hard time getting to sleep that night.

When his mother and father passed by his door on their way to their own room, he was still wide awake, trying not to think about tomorrow.

He did not want to jump off a ladder.

He did not want to leap over the top of a hedge.

Most of all, he did not want to have to face Matt Gordon and his gang again.

At some point during the night he must have fallen asleep, however, because suddenly to his surprise he felt somebody shaking him.

When he opened his eyes, the room was filled with the pale gray light of morning, and Sarah was standing next to his bed with her hand on his shoulder.

"We'd better get going," she said. "It's almost seven."

She looked excited and bright-eyed and well rested.

Brian got out of bed and put on his clothes. Then he packed his superhero costume into his bookbag again. Robbie had suggested that he change into the Wonder Kid outfit at the Chandlers' house since it was right across the street from the school.

When Brian and Sarah went downstairs, their mother was already in the kitchen making coffee.

"Where do you two think you're going?" she asked them.

54

"We have to get to school early today," said Sarah. "We promised to meet some people on the playground."

"You can't go to school without breakfast," their mother said firmly. She poured each of them a bowl of cereal.

Sarah wolfed hers down in half a minute. Brian put a spoonful of cereal into his mouth. He started to chew it.

"Hurry up," whispered Sarah. "We're already running late."

Brian tried to swallow. The cereal would not go down.

"I can't eat when I'm nervous," he whispered back.

Their mother was standing with her back toward them, making peanut butter sandwiches.

Quickly, Sarah stuck her own spoon into Brian's bowl and started shoveling cereal into her mouth.

Their mother got some apples out of the

refrigerator. Then she took a cake out of the cake box and cut two big slices.

Sarah gobbled faster.

By the time their mother had wrapped the cake and sandwiches and put those, along with the apples, into lunch sacks, there was nothing left in either Sarah's bowl or Brian's.

"Can we go now?" Sarah asked eagerly.

"I guess so," their mother said, staring down at the empty bowls. "You certainly must have been very hungry this morning."

Out in the front yard, Brian spat his mouthful of cereal into a rose bush. Then he and Sarah walked hurriedly over to the school grounds.

Robbie and Lisa were there ahead of them. They looked as if they had been waiting for quite a while.

"What took you so long?" asked Robbie. "Lisa and I have been here for ages. We've already brought the ladder over and spaded up the landing field."

The stepladder was set up outside the Sixth-Grade Gate. On it there hung a sign:

DANGER — HEDGE TRIMMERS AT WORK

A pair of clippers lay at the base of the ladder.

"The sign and clippers were my idea," said Lisa. "This way people won't wonder why there's a ladder on the sidewalk."

"You'd better hurry if you want a test jump," Robbie said to Brian. "If we wait any longer, Matt and his gang will be here."

Brian looked at the stepladder. It was a high one. It reached to the very top of the hedge.

Sarah could tell exactly what he was thinking.

"We voted," she reminded him. "It came out three to one in favor."

"I know," said Brian, "but I still don't think this is fair."

He handed his lunch sack to Sarah and placed one foot on the lowest rung of the ladder. Then he stepped up onto the second rung.

"It's shaky," he said. "I think it's going to fall over."

"No, it's not," said Robbie. "It's very well balanced."

Brian slowly climbed to the top of the ladder.

He gazed out across the hedge and then down to the playground below.

"The hedge is too wide," he said. "I'll never clear it."

"Sure, you will," said Robbie. "Remember, Wonder Kid can do anything."

Brian looked down again. He started to feel dizzy.

He closed his eyes and thought about being Wonder Kid. He wished that he were already dressed in the costume. Without it, it was hard to feel like a superhero.

"Hurry up," Robbie said. "We don't have all day!"

Brian braced himself and pushed off from the ladder. Even as he did so, he knew he was not going to make it across.

An instant later he felt his feet hit the hedge. Branches clawed at his body, and twigs scratched his face. Down, down, down he went into the very heart of the hedge. When at last he came to a stop, he felt as if he were being held in place by a million sticks jabbing into him from all directions.

After a moment, he slowly opened his eyes.

All he could see around him was a curtain of green.

9

"Brian?" Sarah's voice called anxiously. "Are you hurt?"

Brian tried to answer, but he could not make a sound. There didn't seem to be any air in his lungs.

"Brian?" Now it was Robbie's voice calling to him. "Are you okay?"

"Please, say something!" begged Lisa. "Tell us you're all right!" She sounded as if she was getting ready to cry.

Brian finally managed to draw in some breath.

"I don't know if I'm all right or not!" he shouted. "I'm stuck halfway down in the middle of the hedge."

"We'll get you out," Robbie said. "We have the hedge clippers. This side is so thick with leaves, though, that I think it might work best if I cut through from the other side."

"I'll go around and check it out," said Sarah. Brian could hear the pounding of her feet as she raced through the gate and out onto the playground.

After a moment, he heard some rustling and snapping. Then Sarah's hands appeared in front of his face. The hands tore at the leaves and branches until they had made a large enough hole so Sarah herself could peer in at him.

"You look funny," she said. "There's a leaf sticking out of your nose."

62

"I don't see anything funny about it," snapped Brian.

"Don't worry," said Sarah. "Robbie will get you out."

She drew her face back from the hole, and Brian glanced past her. What he saw caused him to gasp in horror.

A group of boys was striding toward them across the playground.

"Matt and his gang are coming!" Brian hissed at his sister.

Sarah whirled and jumped away from the hedge.

"Well, look who's here!" said Matt. "It's Wonder Kid's buddy! Where's Superhero today, still getting his teeth cleaned?"

"Wonder Kid will be a bit late," said Sarah. "He had to stop on his way to zap some bank robbers."

"Then it's lucky for you that you brought us lunch," said Matt. "Are those *two* sacks I see on the ground over there?"

"You wouldn't want to bother with those," said Sarah. "There's nothing in them but dry old peanut butter sandwiches."

"That's better than tuna," said Matt. "Isn't that right, guys?"

The boys in his gang burst out laughing, and Brian could hear the rustle of paper. He knew Matt was opening the sacks and unwrapping the sandwiches.

"Hey, great!" Matt exclaimed. "There's chocolate cake in this one!"

"You can't have that!" cried Sarah. "That cake is my brother's! He didn't eat any breakfast, and he'll be starved by lunchtime!"

Brian could not believe what he was hearing. He had never known Sarah to worry about someone else's stomach.

"Yum, yum!" said Matt, making smacking sounds with his lips. "Is there a piece of cake in that other sack too?"

"You're going to be sorry when Wonder Kid gets here!" cried Sarah.

"Don't be silly," said Matt. "You know there isn't any Wonder Kid. That kid in the funny costume was probably your brother. That creep's such a nerd, he could never stand up to anybody."

Brian was swept with a sudden surge of fury. He could not keep his mouth shut a moment longer.

"I'm on my way to Summerfield now!" he shouted. "If you bullies know what's good for you, you'll leave Sarah alone!"

For a moment Matt and his friends were too startled to speak.

Then one of the boys asked shakily, "Who was *that*?"

"That was Wonder Kid!" cried Sarah. "I told you he was coming! He's flying this way, and he's sending his voice ahead of him!"

"That's crazy," said Matt. "You can't project a voice without a phone or a radio."

"A superhero can!" Brian bellowed. "Superheroes have powerful vocal cords! You'd better get out of the way before the rest of me gets there!"

"We do need to hit the road, Matt," said one of the gang members. "If we don't get a move on, we're going to be late for school."

"Chicken!" sneered Matt. "You're nothing but a bunch of chickens! Can't you see this fat twerp is trying to trick us? I bet she has a radio stashed over there in the hedge."

"That wasn't a radio," another boy said. "That was really Wonder Kid talking. I recognized his voice."

"Somebody's cut a hole in the hedge," Matt insisted. "I'm going to look inside and see what's been hidden there."

Brian peered out through the opening in the hedge. He saw Matt coming toward him, and he felt like crying.

He thought about Matt's horrid face getting closer and closer.

He pictured Matt's mean eyes glaring in through the hole.

He decided that when that happened, he would spit in Matt's face. He only wished he still had a mouthful of cereal.

Then, all of a sudden, something astonishing happened. From somewhere above, a voice shouted, "*Look out below!*"

A figure came hurtling down from out of the sky. It was wearing a hood and a cape, and its arms bulged with muscles.

"*Wonder Kid to the rescue!*" cried the boy in the superhero outfit, and an instant later, he crashed right on top of Matt Gordon.

10

Suddenly a lot of voices were yelling at once.

There was so much noise and confusion that Brian couldn't tell exactly what was happening. Sarah had somehow managed to grab the lunch sacks and was waving them wildly about as if they were flags. She was also jumping up and down in front of the hole in the hedge, blocking Brian's view of everything but her back.

Then she hopped to one side, and he could see again.

On the far side of the playground, Matt's friends were racing away.

Brian had never seen boys run so fast.

Matt himself was lying flat on the ground, and standing over him was the powerful figure of Wonder Kid.

"So, you don't believe superheroes can fly?" he cried. "So, you don't believe they can project their voices and leap buildings? At least there's one thing you *have* to believe about superheroes: they always come to the rescue of their friends."

Matt made a whimpering noise like a frightened puppy.

"Please, don't zap me," he begged. "Oh, please don't zap me!"

"Then, repeat after me," said Wonder Kid: "*I believe in superheroes!*"

"I believe in superheroes," Matt responded quickly.

"*I promise I will never snatch anybody's lunch again!*"

Matt said, "I promise I'll never snatch anybody's lunch."

"*And the Sixth-Grade Gate will be free to be used by everybody!*"

"And the Sixth-Grade Gate — " Matt began. His voice broke. "Please don't zap me, Wonder Kid! I have very tender skin."

"Zap him!" Sarah commanded. "He called my brother a nerd!"

"What?" exclaimed Wonder Kid. "Matt called my friend a bad name?"

He raised his right arm into a zapping position.

"I take it back!" screamed Matt. "I didn't know Sarah's brother was a friend of yours! I'll never say anything mean about him again!"

"*And the Sixth-Grade Gate?*" prodded Wonder Kid.

"It will be free to be used by everybody!"

"All right," said the superhero. "I guess I can release you now."

"No, wait a minute!" cried Lisa, appearing out of nowhere. She was carrying a notebook in one hand and a camera in the other. "Before he gets up off the ground, I want to take a picture. I'll need it to illustrate my story for the newspaper."

She aimed the camera at Matt and Wonder Kid.

Wonder Kid pointed his finger as though he were zapping Matt.

Matt just lay in the dirt looking miserable and terrified.

"We'll have to print extra copies of this issue," said Lisa. "Everybody at school is going to want one."

"I'm letting you go now," Wonder Kid told Matt. "I want you to be sure, though, not to forget your promise: *You are never again to take away any kid's lunch.*"

Matt jumped up off the ground and started

running. In a matter of seconds he had disappeared into the school building.

As soon as Matt was out of sight, Wonder Kid rushed to the hedge. He pulled off his hood, and curly red hair sprang out.

"Did you see that wonderful leap I made?" asked Robbie.

"That was only because you've got such long legs," said Brian. He knew it was dumb to be jealous, but he couldn't help it. "Your aim was bad. You didn't come down in the landing field."

"I couldn't see where it was," said Robbie. "I had to take off my glasses. I knew Matt would expect Wonder Kid to have perfect eyesight."

Suddenly the sound of a bell rang out across the playground.

"Oh, no!" cried Sarah. "We're going to be late again!"

"You girls go ahead," said Robbie. "I'll stay here and get Brian out."

74

"We'll all stay," said Lisa. "If we're late, we're late together."

She went back to the sidewalk and returned with the pair of hedge clippers. Within a short time Robbie had widened Sarah's hole enough so Brian could scramble through.

Lisa's eyes widened with horror at the sight of his scratches.

"Do they hurt a lot?" she asked anxiously.

"Not really," said Brian. "My skin must be tougher than Matt's." Then he heard himself saying something that surprised him as much as anyone. "You know, I'm actually going to miss being Wonder Kid. Whenever I put on that costume, I stopped feeling like a nerd."

"You shouldn't *ever* feel like a nerd!" exclaimed Robbie. "After all, you're the one who *invented* Wonder Kid! And he doesn't have to be gone for good, you know. We can always bring him back when there are people who need him."

"We can all take turns being Wonder Kid," said Lisa. "There's no good reason superheroes have to be boys."

"As long as we don't get too fat for the costume," said Brian. At that, everybody turned to look at Sarah.

"Let's vote," said Lisa. "Everybody in favor of keeping Wonder Kid, raise your hand."

The vote came out four to zero in favor of keeping him.

Sarah licked chocolate frosting off her fingers.

"Once a friend, always a friend," she said.

Tin Can
Tucker

LYNN HALL

Tin Can
Tucker

Charles Scribner's Sons / New York

Copyright © 1982 Lynn Hall

Library of Congress Cataloging in Publication Data
Hall, Lynn.   Tin Can Tucker.
    Summary: A sixteen-year-old girl runs away from her
foster home in Missouri, planning to make a name for
herself on the rodeo circuit.
    [1. Rodeos—Fiction   2. Foster home care—Fiction]
I. Title.
PZ7.H1458Ti   1982   [Fic]   82–5891
ISBN 0–684–17623–8   AACR2

1 3 5 7 9 11 13 15 17 19   F/C   20 18 16 14 12 10 8 6 4 2

Printed in the United States of America

Tin Can
Tucker

1

Her name was Ann Tucker, but she went by Tuck, to head off Little Orphan Annie jokes. No middle name. She reckoned the state of Missouri had probably gone to all the bother it wanted to, just coming up with "Ann" and "Tucker." But it didn't matter. She planned to earn herself some more name, rodeoing, like when Larry Mahan got to be World Champion bull rider, and they started calling him "Bull."

She was hoping for something like "Slim" or "Tex," but she knew it was going to have to come natural, from people liking her or respecting her, and as yet all these future friends were still waiting to come into her life. Waiting on down the road.

McAlester.

She grinned and hiked the gym bag onto her other shoulder. Sixty, seventy more miles, and there she'd be. She raised her face to the thin February sunshine and half-closed her eyes as her feet followed the edge of good old Highway 69. Three days now, mostly walking but some-

1

times riding if the ride-offerer looked safe. Tuck Tucker was no fool. She intended to arrive in her new life un-raped, unbeat-up, and unrobbed, so her thumb went out only to cars with families, and since most of them didn't stop, she'd put a good many miles on her Keds these three days. But they were still the best darn three days she'd ever had.

By her own lights Ann Tucker was a long old drink o' water, built like a steel fence post, hair like a rained-on haystack, face like a skillet bottom. The few people who knew her well thought of her much more warmly, and those who were old enough saw in her a Doris Day kind of quality, a scrawny sixteen-year-old Doris Day made up to look dusty and sunburned.

Motor sounds from behind. Tuck walked backward, squinting to see as much as she could as fast as she could, to know whether it was Highway Patrol, a potential ride, or neither. This close to McAlester, and the day before the start of the rodeo, she'd about made up her mind to hold out for a ride that looked like it was rodeo people. And this one . . . might. . . .

It was a pickup with a shell on behind, pulling a little aluminum camping trailer. It looked fairly dusty and beat-up, and there were, yes, two heads inside, man and woman. Tuck upped her thumb. The rig rattled past, slowed, pulled over. Bumper stickers on the back of the trailer said, "Have you hugged your horse today?" and "Rodeo cowboys do it better." Tuck whooped and ran.

A gray haired woman with a well-worn face and some absent teeth leaned out the window and squinted down into Tuck's face. "You're a girl, ain't you?" she bellowed.

2

Tuck stopped in her tracks. The question had never been raised before.

The woman, apparently satisfied on that score, said, "You on drugs or anything like that?"

"Hell, no," Tuck grinned. "I'm just trying to get to the rodeo."

Immediately the door opened, and the woman shoved over to make room. "Can't be too careful these days," she said cheerfully. "Anymore, the ones with the long ponytails is most likely boys, and the last hitchhiker we picked up pulled a knife on us. He passed out about then, though, and we was able to get rid of him, but the experience made us a little cautious, you can imagine. Heading for the rodeo, huh? What you going to do there?"

"Don't know yet." Tuck hung her arm out the window and relaxed in the luxury of going forward while sitting down.

Beyond the woman was a man who grinned around at Tuck as he drove. He was maybe sixty, little, bald, cheerful looking, Tuck thought. She grinned back at him. "You a rodeo rider?" she asked, figuring he was too old but might get a kick out of being mistaken for one anyway.

"I'm a clown, a bullfighter. Name's B.C. Olmstead. This's my bride Grace, here. How 'bout yourself, if you don't mind me asking?"

"Call me Tuck." She hauled her arm in from outside and shook with both of them. "I sure appreciate the ride. Wasn't sure my shoes were going to hold out all the way, and I didn't want to use up my boots, walking."

"Come a long way, did you?" Grace asked.

Tuck pondered for a moment, then decided these

3

weren't the kind of folks who were likely to send a person back to a group home. "From Springfield."

"Hitchhike all that way? On your own?" B.C. peered around his wife. "You must want to get to this rodeo pretty bad. Got a boyfriend there, I bet."

Tuck shook her head. "You two are the oldest friends I'll have at that rodeo."

They rode silently for a while, no one wanting to poke in where they might not be welcome. Tuck turned and looked out at the lake they were driving beside and the San Bois mountains in the distance. Oklahoma was beautiful, she thought. Anywhere that wasn't 1534 Panama Street, Springfield, was beautiful.

B.C. pursued gently. "You a big rodeo fan?"

Tuck nodded. She thought about the pile of western magazines she'd had to leave behind, and the Larry Mahan poster that wouldn't have fit in her gym bag, and all of the library's horse books, all the important bits of her other life.

"Been to lots of rodeos, huh?" Grace asked.

"This'll be my first."

From the corner of her eye Tuck caught the glance Grace threw to her husband. She could feel them deciding she was a camp follower, just one of those cowboy-struck girls that goes to rodeos cruising for dates. Couldn't be wronger, she thought.

But then, they'd have no way of knowing about the fascination that had flickered to life in Tuck from the first time she saw pictures of bucking broncs and found out that there was such a thing as rodeo. They wouldn't know how she had felt last December when she sat, transfixed,

4

through three evenings of National Finals Rodeo on television, how she almost had to hang onto the chair arms to keep from being pulled in through the screen, into the world where Tuck Tucker was meant to be.

And they sure couldn't know about the buckle that pressed against her belly under her tucked-out shirttail.

Again they rode silently while Tuck pondered how much she should tell them. Lord knows I'm going to need all the help I can get, she thought.

"What the situation is," she said carefully, "is that it come to me pretty strong here, the last few months, that rodeoing is how I want to live my life. Now, I don't know yet how I'm going to swing it, I mean the money part, but I reckon if other people can, I can. What do you think?"

This time the look that flashed between the Olmsteads was warm and wry and seemed to hold memories. Then B.C. wiped his face serious and turned himself to the problem.

"You run away from home, did you?"

"Yes and no." He waited for more, so she went on. "I'm a ward of the state. Missouri. I lived in a group home in Springfield, with some people who make their living taking in kids like me. They were okay, they weren't mean or anything, but they're not going to miss me. I reckon what they'll do is cover up the fact that I'm gone for as long as they can, so they'll have my support checks without having to put out for my food and all. This other girl that lived there used to run away every now and then, and she told me that once you get up around my age, so you're old enough to make it on your own, the state really doesn't go to much trouble looking for you."

5

Grace nodded as she absorbed the information, then said, "You got any money at all?"

Tuck brightened. "Hundred and twelve dollars and a half. Baby-sitting money. I spent two and a half so far the last three days, for crackers and peanut butter and oranges, and I've still got plenty of food." She nudged the gym bag with her toe.

Grace and B.C. chuckled. Grace said, "Well, honey, if you can get along that low on the hog, you passed the first test for being rodeo people. We don't have a speck of extra room in the trailer, but you're welcome to bunk in the back of the truck if you want to, till you can find yourself something better. Or till you get tired of it and thumb your way back home." Her eyes twinkled.

"Hooeee!" Tuck toned down her whoop for the sake of their eardrums, but she couldn't keep her palm from banging the truck door. She was over the first mountain! Friends, and a place to live, and half a jar of peanut butter left.

She could hardly breathe for the excitement of turning in at the fairgrounds and seeing the village of trucks, campers, trailers, and horse trailers parked among the trees in the grassy outskirts of the rodeo grounds. To her left were these vehicles; to her right, the arena itself, a pipe-fenced oval in which a tractor was dragging the earth smooth. Along the two long sides of the oval were a covered grandstand and low bleachers. At the far end Tuck could just see the chutes—her heart jumped again—and behind them a maze of stock pens. She hung her head

6

as far out the window as she could get it, flared open her nostrils, and hauled in all the horse-smell and cow-smell and dust she could get.

B.C. found a tree with only one other rig parked under it and stopped. As Tuck stepped out she saw what looked like a turquoise refrigerator with a man coming out of it.

"What the heck is that?"

Grace jumped heavily down from the truck and said, "That's a john. Ain't you ever seen one like that? My, you are a greenie, aren't you?" But her grin and her arm-pat took the insult out of her words. "Take a look back here. See if this'll do you."

While B.C. greeted the man in the neighboring camper, Grace went to the back of the pickup and pulled up the top part of the door, pulled down the truck's tailgate. The shell was fiberglass, with screened and louvered windows on the sides and just enough headroom for sitting up in, but not enough for standing. The floor was covered with elderly carpeting that was probably brown under the road dust, the sun-fade, and the stains.

Grace said, "It ain't no Winnebago, but you're welcome to it if you want to bunk in here this trip. We usually seem to end up with a cowboy or two sleeping in there when they don't win their day money and can't afford motels. You'd ought to have you a sleeping bag, though. Nights are going to be cold for a while yet, and that floor gets awful hard toward morning."

Tuck's face glowed as she stared into that six-by-eight space. Quickly she pitched her bag inside, as though to

7

stake her claim to the territory. "It'll do me just fine, and I thank y'all from the bottom of my boots. Can I pay you rent for it, or something?"

Grace laughed, a beautiful bellow of a laugh. "Bless your bones, thanks for the offer, but it don't cost us nothing, and in our young years me and B.C. was helped out an awful lot by other rodeo folks. We're just glad to give a hand where we can. Tell you what, if you're planning to stay the whole four days of this rodeo, you're welcome to use the truck to sleep in, and if you want to kick in, say, a buck or two a day for groceries, I'll be glad to feed you. You don't want to go along on peanut butter and crackers the whole time."

They shook on the deal. Tuck offered to lend a hand with setting up camp, but Grace assured her the trailer needed no looking to. So after a quick detour to the turquoise refrigerator, Tuck jammed her hands into her jeans pockets and set off to look around. She made herself amble slowly, casually, so it wouldn't show that this was her first rodeo. As two cowboys approached, their heads bent close over some story one was telling, Tuck suddenly turned and sprinted back to the truck to exchange holey tennis shoes for her beloved boots.

She set out again, feeling less vulnerable. A shiny brown and tan pickup came bouncing slowly toward her. She stood aside to watch as it stopped. It was a beautiful rig, with a huge camper hulking over it and a matching brown and tan horse trailer behind. A slim blond girl with over-the-ear ponytails and wire-rim glasses jumped out and, with a more or less friendly glance at Tuck, ran back

8

to the rear of the horse trailer and disappeared inside.

Tuck pulled in her breath and thought, Here it comes. My first real live horse.

Brown haunches appeared, a short brown tail, hind legs booted with bulky green wraps, a chunky barrel, narrow shaven-maned neck, front legs also wrapped in green, and finally a blaze-faced head, a head so short, so fine-muzzled yet so deep through the jaws that it was more triangle than rectangle.

Quarter horse, Tuck told herself wisely. The horse was a feast for her eyes, and she devoured him.

The girl at his head glanced at Tuck, then came over and held out the horse's lead rope. "Would you hold him a minute? I want to check something."

Tuck's, "Sure," was casual, but her fist held the lead rope in a dead man's grip. The girl knelt beside the horse's hind leg and stripped off the leg wraps on both legs, then pinched her fingers up and down the tendons at the back of the legs. The horse extended his muzzle to smell Tuck's arm. She was just reaching to touch the gray velvet nose when the girl reappeared at his head, leg wraps slung over her shoulder.

As she took the rope from Tuck she said, "Thanks. I heard him kicking the trailer door a time or two, just as we pulled in, and I was afraid he might have hurt himself. I guess I'm just getting paranoid about his legs, but with a barrel horse. . . ."

Tuck nodded and grinned, eager to show that she understood. She wanted to say something, to hold the girl's attention for another minute or two and maybe get in a

9

pat on the horse. But a tan and brown car drove up beside them, and the woman on the passenger's side rolled down her window.

The girl went to the car and said, "He's started that kicking in the trailer again, Mom. We're going to have to pad those doors with something. Listen, are you guys going to go...."

Tuck ambled away.

As she approached the arena, the horse population got thicker. Horses stood slack-hipped and dozing, tied to the sides of parked trailers. A few walked or jogged or loped around the outside of the arena, carrying cowboys who slouched in the saddle in perfect closeness with the movement of the animals beneath them. One cowboy loped slowly past Tuck, his head thrown back to drain a beer can.

She watched with an overwhelming hunger, not only to be on a horse but to have grown up on horseback, as these lucky people all obviously had.

She wanted to get her hands on one of them, to feel the warm silky hide she'd fantasized about for so long, to smell the smell of them. She looked around but didn't see any horse whose riders looked approachable, so she headed for the far end of the arena where she'd seen the stock pens.

Beyond the row of boxlike chutes at the end of the arena was a maze of pipe-fenced pens, a double row of square corrals with a center aisle between them. Behind the corrals three huge stock trucks, semis, were parked. The lettering on the trucks' sides said, "Merrill and Company, Rodeo Stock Contractors."

Tuck walked slowly past the pens, unsure of whether

10

she was supposed to be back here, but figuring to stay until somebody ran her off. The first two pens held half-grown calves, forty or fifty of them all told, she guessed. Next were bigger cows, bulls or steers, she wasn't sure which and wasn't about to get close enough to find out. But beyond these were cattle that were overwhelmingly, obviously, bulls. The size of them took her breath away, and instinctively she moved to the far side of the aisle.

Ah. The horses.

She stepped up onto the pipe fence for a better look. Compared to the sleek quarter horse she'd held, these were a shaggy looking crew, dusty and rough coated, but to Tuck they were almost equally wonderful. The smell of them!

This was the biggest of the corrals. Tuck guessed there were probably close to eighty horses in there, standing head-down in the afternoon sunshine. Knowing that these must be the broncs, Tuck was a little surprised that they were so placid. Somehow she'd expected rolling eyes and wild behavior.

One horse, a sort of blue-gray with black mane and tail, sauntered out from the group and stopped near Tuck, but ignoring her. The horse's head drooped, its knees buckled, and it sank with awful slowness to the dust. Tuck stiffened in panic. She looked around for someone to yell at, that a horse was dying.

The horse grunted, rolled over on its back, and with what looked to Tuck like a grin of pure pleasure, began whipcracking its body in a supple-waisted squirm, digging shoulders and hips deep into the dust, its four legs folded, relaxed.

11

Tuck relaxed, too, and flushed at how close she'd just come to making a fool of herself. Darn horse was only scratching.

She stared at the animal lying not ten feet away, offering up this intimate look at its belly. It was a mare. Tuck recognized the soft deflated bag of udder for what it was. The mare lay still for an instant, like a dog asking for a belly-rub, and in that instant the mare's eye caught Tuck's stare and held it. A small electric shock went up through Tuck, a recognition of some sort, like meeting her own eyes in the mirror, something Tuck usually avoided doing. Or like hearing your own voice whispering your own name in the dark, Tuck thought.

The mare rolled up onto her feet and shook herself so hard her dust cloud enveloped Tuck. Then, with her body comfortably talcum-powdered against insects and itches, the mare wandered toward one of the piles of hay lying just inside the fence. She watched Tuck from her nearside eye, but without fear.

Tuck forgot the other horses and set to studying this one. The color was a fascination; Tuck moved along the fence till she was within a few feet of the mare. The head and ears were black. So were the legs from hooves to knees, and so were the bushy, scraggly mane and the moth-eaten looking tail. But the body hair was a smooth mixture of black and white hairs that added up to a kind of slate blue-gray. Although the mare's body was broad and muscular, her legs and feet were trimmer than the other broncs, and the black head was more pleasingly planed, free from between-the-eyes bulges and Roman noses that uglified many of the others in the corral.

"Hey there, pretty horse," Tuck said softly. She inched closer and stuck her arm through the fence. The horse went on eating. Tuck's fingers touched the wiry mass of mane hair. Still the horse continued eating. Her heart pounding now, Tuck thrust her fingers through the mane, through the cave of trapped body-warmth under it, until she was touching actual horse neck.

The mare lifted her head and broke the contact, but didn't move away.

From close behind her a man's voice said, "Better watch it there, sis, that's a mean old bronco you're pettin'. You're likely to draw back a bloody stump."

He was middle-aged, paunchy, leathery-looking, and his expression was blandly pleasant in keeping with his tone. Tuck sensed that his words were just habitual patter for kids who hung around his animals.

"These your horses?" she asked.

"Yep. I'm the stock contractor. Who are you? A tin can chaser, I bet."

Tuck frowned. "What's that mean?"

The man shifted his cigar and grinned. "If you gotta ask, you ain't one. Hey, Harold," he turned away and shouted, "did you get them calves watered? Their tank's about dry." He walked away and Tuck went back to feasting on the closeness of the blue mare.

By late afternoon Tuck began to feel drained and drawn from the emotions of the day. She climbed up into the shady part of the stands and sat sprawled back against the bench behind her. She felt like a strummed guitar string.

13

I did it, she thought. I got away from Springfield and school and the home and that whole part of my life. From now on, this is going to be it.

She looked around her at the tan oval of the arena, at the people around the fringes, all here for a purpose, all knowing who they were and what they were doing here. All having a home of some sort to go back to, between rodeos.

For the first time since last December when the idea to do this had taken hold of her, Tuck was partly afraid. Mostly excited, but partly afraid. Just the little toe of one foot, that was all the hold she had on rodeo life. A temporary bed in the back of a truck, for as long as the Olmsteads felt inclined to offer it. And she'd just now touched her first horse.

"Hell, it's a beginning. What I got to do now is find some kind of job that I can do at every rodeo, so I'm at least making grocery money. That'll be the next step. From then on, I'll find some real profession that I can be working up toward, so I'll really belong and not just be a camp follower. I'll have to find out what-all events a girl can compete in and start learning to do one or two of 'em."

New energy tingled through her. She slapped her leg and got up. Back at the trailer, Grace was cooking supper. Tuck looked in the door, sniffed the food smells, and almost doubled up at the attack of hunger pains that had been masked all day by excitement.

"Come on in, look around," Grace said. "Thought I'd start supper a little early, figured you must be kindie hollow by now." She patted Tuck's stomach and hit the buckle. Grace's eyebrows shot up; she looked up at Tuck to see if she'd hit on something she wasn't supposed to know about.

Tuck said, "Well, I don't reckon you'll rob me in the night," and hiked her shirttail.

The buckle was a silver oval almost as big as a hand. In the center of the ornately carved silver was the figure of a bucking horse, worked in gold and flashing a ruby eye. Although Tuck had always kept the tarnish rubbed off the surface of the buckle, the etched pattern of ropes and curlicues around the edge were highlighted by brown tarnish she couldn't get at.

"Oh, my." Grace doubled down to look at the buckle close up, although she was so short it wasn't all that much of a bend to Tuck's midsection. "Where'd you get that? That's a beauty. Old, too, ain't it?"

"I think so. I've always had it. Whoever left me off for the state to raise left it with me, so I expect it belonged to my daddy. See, I didn't know till just this winter that it was a trophy buckle. I just figured it was some big fancy belt buckle, and when I was a little kid I didn't even know what it was at all. But then on the National Finals Rodeo on television last December they were talking about trophy buckles and showed closeups of a couple of them, so then I knew that's what this one was. See? Look here."

She unbuckled it and swung it out to show the back side, which had been engraved. Most of the lettering was rubbed off though, being right over the top snap on a pair of jeans. All that was left were the top halves of five letters and the bottom halves of four numbers that must have been a year date.

Grace leveled a look up into Tuck's eyes, then went

15

back to poking at the meat in the skillet. "That have something to do with your sudden decision to go rodeoing?"

Tuck sat down in the little booth that filled the front of the trailer. She had some trouble getting her knees up under the table. "Well, yes, in a way. Not so much to go looking for my parents, really. I expect they're dead, and if they're not that means they dumped me, and didn't want me, in which case I don't think I want them. It was more like a feeling that, well, they must have been rodeo people, or my daddy anyway, so that means I come by it naturally. You know what I mean? I mean, all my life I'd get excited every time I'd come across anything to do with horses or rodeos, and knowing my parents were rodeo people, well, that kind of explains me. And it gave me something to belong to. That make any kind of sense to you, Grace?"

The woman nodded.

Tuck relaxed back into the booth and stretched out her weary legs. "Actually, it's a wonder this old buckle stayed with me through all those foster homes and group homes and what not. By rights and logic it seems like somebody would have glommed onto it somewhere along the line, when I was a baby especially. Once I got old enough to know I had it, I hung onto it."

B.C. came back then from his visiting around, and supper was served: salisbury steaks and green beans from cans, instant mashed potatoes, little plastic cups of butterscotch pudding. It was the best food Tuck had ever eaten, bar none.

B.C. said, "I put the word out with a few of the boys that you were needing a sleeping bag, Tuck. I expect we can raise one for you somewhere."

"Y'all are sure going to a lot of trouble for me. Do you do this well by every hitchhiker you pick up along the road?"

B.C. chuckled. "Only the ones that turns out to be rodeo folks temporarily down on their luck. It's been done for us many a time, don't worry."

After a few more bites Tuck said, "What's the B.C. stand for, anyway?"

"Buffalo Chips," he said.

Grace said, "Stands for Bullheaded Cussedness."

"No, now," B.C. said, "she asked a straight question, she deserves a straight answer. It stands for," he leaned closer and whispered, "Brilliant Clownwork."

Tuck nodded and accepted that.

There was room for only one dishwasher at the foot-square sink, but Tuck and B.C. stayed around to keep Grace company while she cleaned up. Then they shifted to folding lawn chairs out on the grass. It was almost dark, and there was a definite chill in the air. Tuck fetched her jacket and sweater from her bag and put them both on.

"Tell me about what you do," she said to B.C. as they settled into the chairs.

A battered van bounced past them, and hands waved at B.C. and Grace from every window. The blond girl rode past on her quarter horse, raised a hand, and called, "Hey, B.C, Grace, how you doing?"

Grace called back, "How'd you do at Topeka?"

"Got day money on all my go-rounds, two firsts, and won the average. Missed you there."

"We was working Carthage that week," B.C. called back.

17

The girl nodded and rode on toward the expensive-looking brown and tan camper.

"Who's that?" Tuck asked.

"Jona Riley. She's a barrel racer. About the top can chaser on the circuit this year. She made Finals last year, came out ninth in the World title, as I recall."

"She looks rich," Tuck said before she thought.

Grace chuckled. "Only by rodeo standards, honey, and don't count it against her. Jona's good people."

B.C. said, "You was asking about my clown work, so I'll tell you."

"He'd've told you even if you didn't ask," Grace muttered.

"See that woman?" B.C. pointed dramatically at the squatty form of his wife. "She was six-feet-five when I married her, but I've had to beat her on the head every time she mouths off, and she's down to five-foot-nuthin' by now."

Tuck grinned and stretched and felt herself opening out to this new family of hers, temporary though they were.

"Now, rodeo clowns come in three varieties," B.C. recited. "You've got your entertainers. All they're there for is to jolly up the crowd, keep things from getting draggy between events or when the arena crew has to move equipment around or some such. Then you've got your barrel men. They work in the ring during the bull riding, and they've got a big padded barrel they can dive into if the bull gets too close. Then you've got your bullfighters. That's me. We work the bull riding event, too, but with-

18

out barrels, so it's the most dangerous kind of clown work. It's the highest form of the art.''

Tuck nodded thoughtfully.

"Y'see," he went on, "with the bronc riding events, you've got your pickup men on horseback, that can get in there and get the riders off the horses after their time is up, but you can't do that with bulls. They're so rank they'd just as soon attack a horse as not. It'd be too dangerous for everybody, mostly the pickup horses. The only way down off a bull is through the air. And bulls being what they are, they'd just as soon gore or stomp those fallen riders before the fellows have a chance to get up and get out of there. So us clowns are in there to distract the bull, get him to chase us instead of the cowboy. See?''

Tuck whistled softly. "I sure hope they pay you enough for that kind of work. Can't think of any other reason a sane man would do it.''

Grace bellowed, but B.C. said with dignity, "Listen, honey, I've been doing this for, what, thirty-some odd years now, and I don't reckon there's one bull rider in this part of the country that don't owe his life to me.''

Tuck started to apologize, but he waved her away good-naturedly. A figure came toward them out of the dark with something bulky over his shoulder. He said, "Somebody here looking for a bone bag?''

"Mason. How you been?'' B.C. waved the man into their circle. "Mason Grassley, this here is Tuck Tucker. She's signed on with us for the time being. You got a bag for her, do you?''

He was the skinniest young man Tuck had ever seen,

19

with an Adam's apple you could slice bread on and an overwhelming nose and an overall kind of appeal that made her take her foot down from the truck bumper and sit up a little straighter.

He dropped the sleeping bag on the ground beside her. "Take a look at it if you want. I don't think it's got fleases or diseases. That old Elvin left it in my camper. You remember him?" He turned to B.C. and Grace. "That bull rider with the scrambled brains that was going down the road with me some last year? I believe he's in jail up around Cody, last I heard, so I don't expect he'll be showing up looking for his bone bag. You're welcome to it till such time as he does show up," Mason said, still not looking directly at Tuck.

She picked up the slick nylon bag and held it across her lap. It felt wonderfully warm and soft and *hers*. "Thank you, Mason. I'm glad to meet you. What do you do?"

"Calf and team roping, little steer wrestling now and then. You a can chaser?"

Tuck grinned. She knew what it meant this time. "No, not yet anyway. I don't have a horse. But I'm going to be something."

Quietly, for her, Grace said, "Tuck's got rodeo in her family, Mason. She's just startin' out."

Through the long evening, cowboys, by ones or twos or bigger bunches, drifted in and out of the Olmstead camp, pausing for a "howdee" or an hour of visiting, catching up on one another's news, and telling B.C. they missed him at Topeka last week. They greeted Tuck easily, ignor-

20

ing her or flirting in an automatic kind of way, or just giving her a friendly look from time to time while they visited.

She loved it.

For as long as she could force her eyes to stay focused, she sat among them sponging up their talk, but finally she couldn't hold up any longer. Her last three nights' sleep had been in two ditches and the back seat of a junked car. She heaved herself up into the truck bed, rolled out the sleeping bag, removed boots, belt, and bra under cover of darkness, and folded herself into her new home. She was in the process of relishing it all when sleep conked her out, and she didn't move a hair till the sun came in the window and hit her in the eyes.

2

It was the most beautiful day Tuck had ever seen—sunny, breezy, crispy, sweater weather, a golden day to be sitting beside a rodeo arena. She'd spent the morning drifting from one good thing to another, visiting the blue roan bronc mare through the stock pen fence, taking a shower in the trailer's tiny bathroom and scrubbing everything from hair to four-day-rotten underwear, wandering among the rigs that had arrived during the night and feasting her eyes on horses horses horses, and finally, just after lunch, watching B.C. construct his clown face.

Now she sat with Grace near the end of the free bleachers, across the arena from the paid-admittance shaded grandstand. These bleachers were low and rattly and friendly and not very crowded. She sat at the end of her board to be close to whatever horses might be parked beside her leg, in an open area near the chutes where riders gathered and milled around. Grace hunched over a lapful of delicate yellow baby yarn that was being cro-cheted into a crib-sized afghan for a grandchild. The yarn snagged on rough finger skin, but the stitches came out perfectly every time, to Tuck's amazement.

The loudspeaker sputtered to life and announced first a welcome to one and all, and then the Grand Marshal's parade. To the recorded swell of "Oklahoma" the parade galloped in, and Tuck jostled Grace's stitches in her excitement. Out front came two men on loping palominos, dripping silver from costumes and tack, the horses' hooves flashing silver paint. The men carried flags, American and Oklahoman, and behind them poured a breathtaking river of horses and riders. Cowboys, Indians on Appaloosas, a dozen girls, a four-donkey hitch pulling a chuck wagon. As the bunch galloped around and around, Tuck found two familiar faces: Jona the barrel racer and Mason the bone-bag bringer. His horse was so beautiful that Tuck's breath caught at the sight of him. He was a dark metallic gold buckskin, heavily dappled with circles of brighter gold, and set off by black legs, tail, and the pencil-line black of his shaved mane.

The parade ended with a lineup the length of the arena, facing the paid-for seats, and a hats-off salute to the flag while Oklahoma music gave way to the national anthem. Then, as abruptly as they'd come, the riders left the arena empty for the first event.

Calf roping. Tuck splayed her feet on the bench below and propped her elbows on knees to hunch forward and catch every second of the action. And there weren't many seconds. It thrilled her to see how fast and slick it all worked. The calf came jumping out of the little holding chute, and a fraction later the horse and rider exploded through a rope barrier from another little holding pen, rider already swinging out his loop, and horse leaping after the calf with such speed and precision, such expert placing of himself with the calf, that Tuck wanted to cry for the beauty of the work.

The rope would sing, and catch or miss. When it caught, the cowboy was already on the ground and running along the rope while the horse was jamming back, half-sitting, to hold that rope taut. Cowboy'd grab the calf by legs or leg and flank, maybe give him a knee-lift to get him off balance, and bring him down in the dust. Then with deft whips the cowboy would wrap his pigging string around three of the calf's feet and stand up, throwing his arms in the air to signal the finish. Then the cowboy would remount, listening for his time to be announced and watching to be sure the calf didn't fight loose before the six-second time limit, which would disqualify the rider.

Mason was the sixth rider out. Tuck watched as hard as she could. In three leaps the buckskin laid Mason into his shot, and one breath later the calf was down and the arms were up.

"Yaay," Tuck yelled, just like he really was a friend of hers.

"Time for the cowboy," the announcer drawled, "eleven seconds even. That's the time to beat, this go-round. Let's show him what you think of that ride, folks." Applause.

Suddenly Mason himself was beside Tuck, seeking the shade of the bleacher-end for his horse. He maneuvered the sweating animal alongside Tuck, and he more or less looked at her but didn't say anything.

"Congratulations," she said.

"Thanks."

He pulled his knees up beside the saddlehorn, to hold his elbows up, and pulled his hat deeper over his eyes. He seemed to be settling in to watch the rest of the ropers. Tuck dropped her hand to the horse's neck and stroked it. No one seemed to mind, or even notice.

"What's your horse's name?"

"That's Coppertone," Mason said. "He's a pretty decent little calf-roping horse. I've been working him in team roping and steer wrestling some this last winter, too, and he's coming on real well, but calf roping is his specialty."

They listened for the next announced time. Seventeen point thirty-two seconds.

"How do you know when to start out of your chute?" Tuck asked.

Mason pointed with the ends of his reins. "You see that chalk line in the dirt there, about ten feet out from the chutes? See that fellow standing there with the red flag in his hand? That's the scoreline flag judge. He watches that line, and if the horse comes through his barrier before the calf crosses that scoreline, he raises his flag, and it's a ten-second time penalty. You get a good horse like this one, and he pretty much times his jump-out himself."

Tuck pondered and watched for a while, then said, "If you win this, do you get money?"

"Oh, sure. First place today would be somewhere around three hundred dollars, on down to maybe eighty for fourth place. You call that day money, see, and then at the end of the rodeo—like, this is a four-day rodeo, so

25

we'll have four go-rounds—the calf roper with the best average time for the four trips wins the average, and that'd be maybe a thousand, fifteen hundred. Depends on how much there is in entry fees and added money. See?"

Tuck's eyes widened. "Wow. You can really make bucks doing this, can't you?"

For the first time, his face broke into a grin, and Tuck melted inside. "If you're good, and lucky, you can about make enough to get on down the road to the next rodeo. Gas costs an arm and a leg anymore, and a big old pickup camper and horse trailer don't go past very many stations. And this old boy goes through a bag of Omaline just about as fast." He dropped his hand to Coppertone's shoulder and gave it a light smack.

Tuck squinted and said casually, "If you were, say, a girl, and you were just starting out in rodeo, what would you get into to try to make a living?"

He snorted. "I'd marry a rich bull rider, if there was such a thing, and then wait for him to break his neck and make me a rich widow." He glanced at her. "You're serious, aren't you? Well, in that case, if you wanted to compete in rodeos, about the only thing to do would be barrel racing. That's the only event women are allowed in. You can team-rope, but only if you have a man teammate, and that takes years of practice. And a top horse. Of course, chasing barrels takes a top horse too, and considerable practice, and even then you don't make much at it. But that's about all there is in PRCA rodeos."

"What's that?"

"Professional Rodeo Cowboys Association. This is a

PRCA rodeo. You've got them, and you've got amateur rodeos, and GRA. That's Girls' Rodeo Association. In Girls' Rodeo you can do all the events, riding rough stock and all, but the prize money isn't enough to cover medical expenses, and there aren't very many rodeos. Amateur rodeos, they don't pay enough in prize money to be worth going to, either. The PRCA is your best bet if you're serious about rodeoing, and that kind of narrows it down to barrel racing, I guess."

"Which is hard to do without a horse," Tuck muttered.

The calf roping ended, and Mason Grassley of Wildorado, Texas, was announced winner.

All through the bareback bronc riding, Tuck's mind was divided between watching the broncs and wrestling with the apparently impossible problem of getting from broke beginner, girl-type, to solid rodeo professional.

She watched each bronc that exploded from the chutes to see if it was her blue friend. It never was.

The steer wrestling was exciting to watch, especially Mason's run, which ended badly. He dove off his horse in good time and got his arms around the bull's head and horns like he was supposed to, and dug his heels into the dust, and twisted and twisted. Bull refused to be thrown over.

"Rubberneck," Grace commented. "There's a few of them bulls, it seems like you can twist till who laid the rail, and they just don't ever go down. Mason drew himself a bad one this time."

After steer wrestling, and before the supper break,

came barrel racing. Tuck forgot her numb rear end and aching back muscles and sat forward again as the arena men rolled into place the three oil drums, painted red, white, and blue, in a triangle pattern.

The only event they let women do, huh, she muttered silently. Don't seem fair. How do they expect us to ever make a living at it, that way? Wonder who makes up these rules, anyhow. Sure thing it ain't the women. Well, let's see what there is to this barrel racing.

The announcer boomed, "First up, number sixty-one, Barbara Bates, Hinton, Texas. Fifty-eight on deck."

From the alleyway gate at the end of the arena a dark low-built horse exploded into view, ridden by a whooping, arm-flailing madwoman. Before Tuck could get focused on them, horse and rider had whipped around the right-hand barrel and were shooting across the arena straight at Tuck. Around the left-hand barrel in front of Tuck's bleachers the horse plowed, so close that the rider's shinguard hit the barrel and rocked it. Off again, leaping toward the third barrel at the apex of the triangle and around it in a turn that Tuck could see was too wide, too clumsy. Then they shot for home, the arena entrance with its electric eye timer.

"Time for Barbara Bates, twenty-one and oh four five. Next up, Jona Riley, Liberal, Kansas, number fifty-eight. Fifty-six on deck."

The gleaming chestnut quarter horse Tuck had almost touched last night flew into the ring and laid into the turn around the first barrel. The girl's twin ponytails stood out in the air under her hat as she and the horse churned up out of the turn and pelted toward the next barrel. Another neat turn, another burst of speed, and the final barrel. The horse lay so close to the ground, rounding the barrel, that Jona's boot touched dirt, but the girl remained straight upright. In the homestretch run, Jona had her feet out of the stirrups and into her horse's flanks, and her bat hand beat a rhythm on the horse's rear with every leap. The crowd applauded as horse and rider disappeared into the alleyway, still going like scalded cats.

"Time for Jona Riley, seventeen point three two four. That's the time to beat so far, folks. Next up, number fifty-six, Chris Rausch, Humansville, Missouri. Forty-nine on deck."

Tuck sat forward and studied each run, on the off chance she might be doing it someday, but the longer she watched the more depressed she got, thinking about what Mason had said about barrel racing being the only way a girl could win money rodeoing. Oh sure, it was fine for those girls out there, with their daddies to buy expensive quarter horses for them, buy pickup campers and horse trailers and all that, and support them while they practiced their barrel racing at home between rodeos. But for Tuck Tucker? Might as well shoot for being president of the world; it was just about as likely.

She thought about the group home waiting back there to swallow her up again. She thought about her new home; her bone bag in the back of Olmsteads' pickup, and the beginnings of friends here, and this portable home that was going to shift from town to town but still hold the center of it together, Grace and B.C. and the rest of them

29

that would be her family if she could stick it out long enough. No. No way she was going to let go of what little hold she had on things here.

Before the end of the barrel racing Tuck excused herself from Grace and started out on her grim search. First she went behind the chutes and looked till she found Merrill, the stock contractor. He was lounging back against a pipe fence, chewing his cigar and catching his breath. Nothing much for him to do during barrel racing.

"Hi, sis. How ya doing?" It was an automatic murmur, not a real question, but Tuck answered it anyway.

"How I'm doing is I'm broke and looking for a job. Can you use any help? Temporary or permanent, whatever you need."

He lowered his eyelids and grinned at her around the cigar. "You had a lot of experience handling stock?"

"Never tried it, but I can learn anything, and I really need a job."

"Tell you what. . . ."

Tuck's heart thumped with hope.

"You run on home, put on some lipstick, nice short skirt, little perfume behind the ears. Then you come back and smile at a few of those cowboys hanging around behind the chutes there. Pick out one that's on a winning streak, and you won't have to worry about a job, at least not while the money holds out. Now, doesn't that sound like more fun than chasing cows in and out of pens?"

"Now look." Tuck's eyes glittered. "If I was a man, come asking for a job, you'd say you had a job or you didn't. I'd like the same courtesy, please." Her voice was low and hard.

Merrill's expression went from surprised to embarrassed with a little grin mixed in. "You said a mouthful there, sis, and I apologize. Blind fence post could see you ain't one of them kinds of girls." Tuck wasn't sure she liked that, either. "But I still don't need any help. I got two sons and a son-in-law working for me, and I can't very well fire any of them. Try at the arena office, why don't you?"

She found the arena office under the grandstand, but nobody was in it. The smell of popcorn and roasting hot dogs pulled her down the way to the long, yellow-lit counter of the refreshment booth. The hundred and twelve and a half dollars was wadded deep in her jeans pocket under a fistful of disintegrating Kleenex, and the hunger in her belly was acute, but she hauled her attention away from the mountain of yellow popcorn in the machine, the rack of weiners sweating and spitting and bursting their skins on the grill. She waited till she caught the eye of the one adult behind the counter, a straggle-haired heavyset woman in a soiled apron.

"Could you use any help?" Tuck asked. "I'm looking for a job."

The woman stared at her with absolute absence of expression for several seconds, then said, "Come on back here," and motioned with her head toward the back entrance, through the kitchen and into the booth itself.

"What's your name?"

"Ann Tucker."

"Okay, Ann, tell you what, supper break's about to start. That's our busy time. You wrap this here apron around you and go out there and start learning where

31

things are and what the prices are. If you can survive the supper rush, you can work the stands after that. Two bucks an hour, straight cash, no withholding. If you get any tips they're yours, but you probably won't. It's not that kind of place. You can eat a little if we're not too busy and if you don't pig up all the profits. That okay with you?"

"Yes!" It was all Tuck could do not to hug the woman.

For a fleeting moment Tuck regretted the loss of the evening. This wasn't exactly the way she'd expected to spend her first rodeo night, and she ached to be able to watch the evening performance. But first things first.

Two teenagers, a boy and girl, worked the counter while the woman oversaw the cooking part of the operation. There was no time for getting acquainted. Tuck threw them a broad smile as she tied on an apron that went twice around her skinny hips and turned her attention to finding out where things were and how much they cost.

People began arriving in twos and threes and family groups. Working as swiftly as she could, Tuck wrapped hot dogs and maidrites in squares of white paper and exchanged them for money, made change, learned how to work the handles on the pop machines so that she didn't run foam over onto her fingers any more than necessary. The intensity of the concentration carried her through the two hour time gap between the afternoon and evening performances.

Toward the end, business let up, and she was able to ease up onto a stool and maneuver a loaded maidrite into her mouth. The glory of that food hitting her hollow stomach was like no glory she'd ever known, the food and

32

the knowledge that she was up to a hundred and sixteen dollars.

When the evening performance began Tuck was outfitted with a big cardboard tray that hung around her neck and held twelve boxes of popcorn and six cups each of coke and orange. Her boss, whose name she didn't even know, hooked a change-maker onto Tuck's belt, necessitating the tucking in of shirttails and the exposing of the big silver buckle. If the woman noticed it she made no comment.

"Get up there and sell," the woman said, aiming Tuck toward the grandstand stairs, "and don't be afraid to use your voice. And keep watching the crowd so you don't miss anybody that's trying to get your attention."

It was all Tuck could do to turn her back on the arena, where some sort of wild west act was going on, and climb the grandstand stairs in slow motion, calling "Popcorn, soda pop, popcorn." What she wanted was to sit down, bury her own hands in a box of popcorn, and feast her eyes on the show.

Mostly people ignored her or craned their necks to see around her, but here and there a hand went up in the crowd, and she passed two or three boxes down the line, waiting to collect the money that came bucket-brigading back to her and to send change along from patient hand to patient hand.

Gradually she became aware of a big, warm liking for these people, all sitting there having a good time and spreading their cheerfulness to the people around them and even to her. She returned it with grins and wisecracking answers to the jokes that came her way.

One man, accepting his white and red striped boxes

from her, said, "Don't you get hungry for some of that popcorn yourself, smelling it all night like that?"

When she admitted she did, he passed back fifty cents of the change she gave him and said, "Here you go. Have one on me."

She grinned and accepted. "Thanks. You're a prince."

The man's wife hooted, "Here Prince, here Prince."

The evening got better and better. At twilight the arena lights came on, adding glitter highlights and shadow excitement to the scene. Tuck went back again and again to the refreshment stand for refills, and now and then a tip went into the jeans pocket, to sift down through the shredded Kleenex and add itself to Tuck's survival treasury.

Between selling and watching for buyers in the stands, Tuck managed to watch a fair amount of the bull riding, enough to bring her close to screeching several times, as B.C. in his clown outfit played fast and loose with a ton of furious red-eyed Brahman.

When the saddle bronc riding started, Tuck worked her way down to ground level and hung around near the chutes, watching for her blue roan friend. As the second rider was out and the third was hunkering over his bronc in the chute, dropping his funny looking hornless saddle onto the animal's back, Tuck caught sight of the blue mare trotting wild-eyed down the alleyway in front of the hazing arms of Merrill's relatives. The mare went into the fourth chute like she knew her way to church, and the gate slammed behind her. Tuck knew better than to get into that alleyway for a close-up talk with the mare, not with number five horse already careening toward the chutes.

Instead, she shoved up close to the arena fence between two cowboys with numbers safety-pinned to their backs.

One of them spat. "No day money for this ole boy tonight, that's for sure." He sounded disgusted.

"Bad draw?" the other one asked.

"Yeah. That Blue Blazes dink. Can't buck for sour apples. Well, best be getting ready for my canter in the park."

When he'd left Tuck said to the one who was left, "Why's he so mad? Isn't he less likely to get thrown off a horse that can't buck for sour apples?"

The man was shorter than Tuck but built so tough he managed to give her the feeling of being hovered over anyhow. Patiently he said, "No, see, you've got two judges out there. Each judge can give a total of up to twenty-five points to the rider for how good he rode, *and* up to twenty-five points for how good the horse bucked. So if you draw a horse like this roan jughead that does more running than bucking, you're going to lose a mess of points no matter how good a ride you give it. See? Nobody likes to draw a horse like that; it purely takes the heart out of a bronc rider, knowing he's beat before he starts."

Tuck nodded wisely. It hurt her to have one of her precious few new friends called a dink and a jughead, but she couldn't very well say so, especially since the guy was probably right. She swung her tray around to her hip so she could belly up close to the fence.

The third rider was just doing a flying dismount over

35

the rump of the pickup man's horse as his bronc made its way across the arena in petering-out hops to where the second pickup man caught it and led it away.

"Fourth up now, folks, number five twenty-one, Randy Goff of Tyler, Texas, on Blue Blazes."

Tuck sucked in her breath.

The chute door swung wide and her mare was out of there, head down, bucking fine as far as Tuck could tell— for the first few bounds anyway. Then the horse kind of strung herself out, some bucking, some running, toward the far end of the arena. Her rider flailed at her with his spurs. A second or two before the buzzer sounded to end the eight-second ride, the mare slowed to a trot.

As though she herself were being ridiculed, Tuck's ears turned red in the roar of good-natured derision that came down from the grandstand. As Randy rode back behind the pickup man, one of the railbird cowboys yelled, "Hey, Randy, was you singing that horse a lullaby out there? She's about ready to go nighty-bye, looked like."

Randy called back, "I have that effect on all the females." But Tuck could see he was mad, under the joking.

By ten o'clock the rodeo was over and the refreshment stand turned off and locked up. "Can you use me again tomorrow?" Tuck asked as she exchanged apron for wages.

The woman pondered. "You did a good job tonight. I reckon we can use you tomorrow if we get much of a crowd. Come around about one and we'll see."

Tuck said, "How about after this rodeo is over? Will you be at the next one?"

"Nah. We're local. We just work this stand whenever something's going on out here. We're here every Tuesday

36

night for the stock car races though, if you want to work then."

"No. That's okay. I'm with the rodeo." Tuck took her new ten dollars and the box of leftover popcorn her boss gave her at clean-up time and wandered away.

So much for steady employment. Still and all, three more days of it would allow her to make a contribution to B.C.'s gas money when she asked if she could ride with them to the next rodeo, and it would buy a few groceries and keep her hundred and twelve and a half dollars intact for now.

It's better than a poke in the eye with a sharp stick, she decided, and headed back toward the stock pens for one last look at her friend, the dink.

The mare stood, head down and dozing, a little apart from the other broncs. Even in the semi-dark the mare's distinctive coloring was easy to spot. Tuck glanced around, saw no one close enough to notice what she was doing, then stuck her hand, with a fistful of popcorn, through the fence toward the mare.

"Here, girl," she called softly. "Got something for you."

The mare approached.

"Don't feel bad," she murmured as the mare came close and began to lip at the popcorn. "I been called a dink a few times myself, or just the same as. It doesn't neces-sarily mean you're no good, only that you don't happen to be doing things like other people think you should. But hell, they're not always a hundred percent right. Look at me, here in McAlester at a rodeo on a Thursday when by rights I should have been taking a history test and playing volleyball on the Blues team in P.E. See, that's what other people think I should be doing. But I know me better than they do, so I did something about it, and here I am. Maybe you don't think you're supposed to be a saddle bronc, and you're doing something about it. Huh? Huh? Want a little more? That's pretty good stuff, isn't it?"

In the end it was the mare who finished off the last little bits of salty popcorn from the crevices of the box bottom.

3

"Come on," Tuck wheedled, "tell me what the B.C. really stands for."

The three of them were enjoying a leisurely breakfast in the trailer's dining booth, hash brown potatoes with runny fried eggs on top, and Canadian bacon and V8. Grace spent more time standing up to stir and serve than sitting, but since she didn't seem to mind, Tuck relaxed and quit offering to help.

B.C. said, "Okay, I'll tell you. Beauregard Charlemagne."

"Oh it does not," she scoffed.

Grace said, "Stands for Before Christ. That's when he was born."

Tuck saw she wasn't about to get a straight answer from either of them, so she turned her energy toward her plate. Eating had never been as exciting as these last couple of days, she thought, maybe because now every bite she took she'd earned and paid dearly for. Or maybe it was the high she was living in, having made her dream come true, or maybe it was all the outdoor fresh air.

It had been a late night last night, with friends of Grace's and B.C.'s dropping in and wandering away, sometimes bringing a bottle of something to drink or a guitar. Tuck had stayed awake this time till the last cat was hung, somewhere around two in the morning, and she'd loved every minute of it—the cowboys' brags or excuses about their performances that day, and all the other nonsense talk that went on. Lots of it was over Tuck's head, either names of people she didn't know or insiders' rodeo slang, but sitting close to Grace's chair she'd felt that she belonged anyhow, and not always knowing what they were talking about was all right, for now.

She'd gone to bed as late as the rest of them, stretched out in her bone bag in the back of the pickup, her head on her gym-bag pillow, her feet flat against the tailgate, her flesh flattening to accept the hardness under the bag's stuffing. And she'd slept till nearly nine, like Grace and B.C.

/ Today looked like less of a thrill than yesterday. Kill time till one, then see if she had a refreshment stand job for the day, then probably do that all the rest of the day. Oh well, still better than Springfield and a day in school.

Grace finally sat down to her own plate. "Not wanting to pry or anything, Tuck, but what do you reckon to do from here on? You still got schooling to finish, don't you? What kind of plans you cooking up for yourself?"

Tuck blew out a long sigh. "That's the big question. I had a little over a year yet to go. I was a junior this year, but I've got extra credits. I kept signing on for extra work, just, I don't know, trying to push through school so I could get out on my own as soon as I possibly could. And not being loaded down with dates and all that, nor any more

40

family life than you could put in a pig's ear, well, I just took extra classes. I had some sort of notion of leaving home this summer, skipping my senior year which I had already done most of the semester hours to get graduated anyway, and then taking one of those tests that you can take and get your high school diploma. Equivalency tests, or whatever they call them. I reckon I'll still do that, but I might have to take some extra courses or something, somewhere along the line."

"But you are going to get your high school diploma," Grace said, sounding like a mother.

Tuck nodded and slugged down her juice. "I have to have that. Mostly I just don't want to be the kind of person who didn't even graduate from high school. You know?"

"Sure," B.C. said. "You've got to face yourself in the mirror every morning when you shave."

"Stop that." Grace kicked at him.

Tuck grinned. This was the kind of family she'd always wanted and never reckoned to have.

Grace said, "Well then, why did you take off when you did, and how come you to head out for McAlester? I mean, I know you were looking for a rodeo, but. . . ."

"It was seeing the National Finals on television, and knowing all of a sudden that my buckle was a rodeo buckle, and, well, like I told you, I suddenly knew that I was a rodeo person, and I couldn't waste any more of my life being in the wrong place. I was always reading the *Western Horseman* magazines in the library, well, all the horse magazines, but that one listed coming rodeos, and I just picked out one that was close enough to get to, hitchhiking, but not so close that anybody from the state would come looking for me. Like if there'd been a rodeo right there in Springfield, somebody probably would have thought to look for me there. And this one being a four-day rodeo I had hopes. . . ." She stopped, confused, then went on. "I had hopes I could maybe find somebody to hook up with, you know, that I could get on down the road with."

She faded to a near-whisper at the end, for fear of having said too much.

Grace patted her knee, and B.C. hooted, "Well, you found somebody. Long as you chip in for the groceries and don't go to getting drunk and disorderly, you're welcome to the family, kiddo."

Tuck's throat swelled shut a minute. When she could talk she said, "I want to chip in on the gas, too, on the road."

"All donations cheerfully accepted." B.C. stood up, stretched, scratched, and wandered outside.

"Grace?"

"Yeah?"

"Come on now, what does it really stand for?"

"Stands for Born Cussed, honey."

First thing after breakfast Tuck went to the stock pens to visit her blue friend. The barrel racing barrels were set in place in the arena, and several of the girls were taking turns running them, working on the rough spots in last night's performances, Tuck figured. She watched out of the corners of her eyes, not wanting to stop and stare and let her hunger show.

At the stock pens she halted in surprise. The blue

mare was in a roped-off corner of the pen by herself. Mr. Merrill was working nearby with one of his relatives, throwing hay in for the other horses.

"Doesn't she get any?" Tuck yelled, pointing to the blue mare.

"Kill buyer's coming to pick her up this morning," he yelled back. "No sense wasting good hay on her."

Tuck marched over to him. "What do you mean, kill buyer? You going to have that perfectly good horse killed?"

He paused, chawed his cigar out of the way of his words, and explained. "Perfectly good is stretching it considerable in this case, sis. You see her buck last night?"

"Yes."

"Then you're the only one who did. Rest of us saw her taking a cowboy for a nice little canter through the park. She just ain't rank enough to make good bucking stock. And she's got time-wise. Not much you can do with them when they get time-wise. She knows when the eight seconds is just about up, and she slows down. That Randy come after me last night fit to nail my hide to the wall because of that mare, and I don't blame him. No sir, not one bit. He paid twenty dollars he didn't hardly have in entry money, and he's a good bronc rider. On a decent horse he'd have scored well enough to at least get back his entry fee. But that mare cost him sorely, and got him laughed at to boot. How long do you think I'd stay in this business if I let that happen very often?"

"Well yes, but just because she's no good at bucking, that's not saying she's a totally worthless horse. You've got no call to kill her over it. Give her to me."

She said it without thinking, but as soon as the words

43

were in the air, Tuck meant them like she'd never meant anything before in sixteen years.

Merrill's hand descended like the weight of the world onto Tuck's shoulder. "Now don't go getting all upheaved about this. Sure, she might be able to be retrained, maybe make a saddle horse of some kind, but it'd take a hell of a lot of time and patience, and she ain't a thing out of the ordinary that anybody'd want to go to all that trouble over. She's not no quarter horse, nor anything fancy; you can see that for yourself. And the kill buyers are paying sixty cents a pound, on the hoof. That's close to six hundred dollars I can turn on her just by making one phone call. Which I already made, and here comes the truck now."

He turned to break open a hay bale.

"Well *I* like her, and *I'd* take the trouble to retrain her." Tuck walked around in front of him, where he had to look at her. "Would you sell her to me?"

Merrill straightened up again and studied her. "You got five hundred dollars, you can have her. I'll take a little loss. Hell, I don't like to send them to the kill market any more than the next man. But I've got to get my investment out of her, too. You understand that. Five hundred, she's yours."

Tuck stiffened. She was in up to her neck now. There was one . . . but she couldn't . . . but the mare was standing there looking sadly over the rope barrier at the other horses eating. And the truck driver was saying, "Hey, Merrill, which one is it? Let's get it loaded."

"Wait." Tuck hauled up her shirt tail and fumbled

44

with the buckle. "Would you take this? It's worth a lot of money."

When he saw what she was doing, Merrill got a look on his face that told Tuck that trophy buckles probably got traded and pawned quite a bit by rodeo cowboys in money trouble and that Merrill wasn't going to be too impressed by hers. But when she finally managed to get it unhooked and unsnapped from her belt and handed it over, the man's expression changed.

"This is a real antique," Merrill said, rubbing his thumb over the design and squinting at the ruby in the horse's eye. "Where'd you get it?"

"I think it was my father's. It was left with me when I was a baby." It sounded like a made-up story even to her, like a bad movie plot, but she looked him in the eye and he believed her.

The truck driver motioned to the mare. "That the one?"

"Hold it a minute," Merrill said. "This must mean a lot to you, sis. You don't really want to trade this for a worthless, flunked-out bronc, now."

"No, I don't *want* to, but I don't see as I have much of a choice," she snapped. "You're bound and determined to get your money out of her, and I'm bound and determined she's not going to be horsemeat." She raised her voice and threw it at the truck driver. "So if you'll take the buckle, I'll take the horse. Is it a deal?"

Merrill squinted and rubbed his jaw, making a sandpaper sound of callus against whisker stubble. At length he said to the driver, "I'm sorry there, Johnson. I guess I

45

called you out on a false alarm. Got a buyer here for the animal. You bill me for your trip out anyway, and sorry for taking your time."

Tuck sagged against the fence.

"Tell you what, sis," Merrill said. "I got a notion you'd feel pretty bad about losing this buckle permanent, and I ain't nearly so heartless as you might think if you listen to gossip. I'll hang onto this here buckle for, what, say six months. That sound fair to you? If you can come up with the five hundred by then you can have your buckle back. Otherwise I'll have to sell it."

Tuck's breath came back, and her spirits shot up and out of sight. The horse! And the buckle not completely lost! She let out a whoop that startled the broncs away from their hay and on impulse grabbed Merrill and hugged the cigar right out of his mouth.

"It's a deal." She cleared her throat, picked up his cigar and dusted it off on the seat of her jeans and handed it back to him. He stuck it back in his mouth.

"Now," Tuck said, "I think we ought to put this down in writing, don't you? Just to keep things straight and legal. And we'll need a couple of witnesses, disinterested third parties, isn't that what they call them? How about those two cowboys over there? They any relation to you?"

Merrill bellowed out a laugh and dropped his arm around her shoulder as they started toward his truck-cab office. "Hell, sis, it's an experience doing business with you. I won't quite say pleasure, but I will say experience. Hey, Jack, Buck, come here a minute. We need you to witness a business transaction here, between sis and me."

Fifteen minutes later Tuck was leading her horse across the back side of the rodeo grounds. Her horse! Her belt ends flapped, and her stomach missed the feel of the buckle, but the blue roan mare was alive and well and plodding beside Tuck's shoulder. They went around the back part of the grassy parking area to avoid the congestion near the arena. Tuck was leery of her horse's behavior, out like this being led like an ordinary horse instead of being herded from here to there with the other broncs. But the mare moved quietly, looked around with interest, paused for snatches of grass every now and then. She wore a faded nylon halter that Merrill threw into the bargain along with the twenty feet of rope she'd been cornered with in the corral.

Another reason Tuck took the long way home was that she had no idea what the next step was, nor how Grace and B.C. were going to feel about all this.

Or how on God's green earth she was ever going to take care of the horse and get it transported to the next rodeo, and the next, and on down the road.

"You and I might be hitchhiking together, old girl." Tuck stretched her finger up from the halter she held, and ran it along the little moleskin lumps of the mare's face by the corner of her mouth. "But don't you worry. I'm going to find some way of taking care of the both of us. You're my family now, and I'm yours. We may be a couple of dinks to the rest of the world, but that's just because they don't know us yet, huh? Huh? We'll show 'em. If we can just figure out some way of not starving in the meantime."

Mason appeared, riding toward her on Coppertone. Tuck saw no movement of his hands on the reins, but the

47

buckskin halted beside her. Mason's long, homely face was half hidden in the shadow of his hat, but his mouth quirked up in a smile. Tuck braced for his derision.

"What you got there?"

"Elephant. I'm joining the circus." Beat him to the punch.

He pushed his hat back. "That's that Blue Blazes horse, isn't it? That dud of Merrill's? What you doing with it?"

Tuck stepped back and dropped one arm protectively over her horse's neck. "I bought her. Merrill was going to have her butchered just because she's not a good bronc, so I bought her instead. I'm going to try to retrain her."

Interest kindled on his face. "No bull. Hey, I want to watch that little job. You ever done any bronc riding?"

"Never been on a horse," she said shortly and continued walking. He reined Coppertone around beside her.

"You kidding me? How could you live to be . . . however old you are, and not even been on a horse?"

"It wasn't from lack of wanting to," she snapped.

The horses' hooves made a soft plopping rhythm in the dust of the parking area as they moved closer to the arena. Tuck was glad to have Mason along, but she was mostly concentrating on her horse, watching for signs of trouble. The mare continued to move placidly.

"She seems pretty quiet," Mason observed. "Maybe you won't have too much trouble riding her. Outside of the arena, and without an association saddle and flank strap, she might not buck too much at all. Heck, she never bucked much even when she was supposed to." He laughed, saw Tuck wasn't laughing, cleared his throat, and got quiet.

"How you going to manage?" he asked abruptly. "You're not overly weighted down with money, as I understand it. What are you going to do with her when the rodeo ends?"

"Try to find somebody that can haul her to the next one for me." Tuck squinted up into the sun and Mason's face. "You know anybody that might?"

He shrugged. "I could probably haul her for you."

As easy as that, the first big problem fell away.

Grace accepted the advent of the mare with mild interest that deepened to concern when she heard what the trade-off had been. "Oh honey, you don't want to lose that buckle. No horse'd be worth that. I mean considering how you came to have it and all. Well, we'll see what B.C. thinks when he gets back from wherever he's wandered off to. Here, let's bring her over here and tie her to this tree so she can eat and have shade. My, she's a pretty color, ain't she? And she seems nice and quiet for a bronc. Well, she was a saddle bronc, wasn't she? They're not quite so rank as those bareback horses are. They can just be ornerier than two tomcats in mating season."

Tuck tied the horse with a triple knot, then stood back to feast on the animal and savor the ownership. With a, "Be right back," Mason rode off and returned a half hour later with a black rubber stable bucket balanced on his leg. He handed it down to her and dismounted.

"I went scrounging for you. Guy was throwing out this old bucket because it was bent out of shape, but I bent

49

it back. And here's a rubber curry comb, handle's broken is all, and a brush. Some bristles gone along this one side, but you can get some good out of it anyhow. You'll probably need to buy you a bridle or hackamore of some kind when you start riding her. I couldn't come up with anything like that, but I'll keep my eyes open."

Tuck accepted the offered treasures.

"You want a quick riding lesson?" Mason said suddenly. "I've got a little time."

"You'd let me ride him?" She glowed, looking at Coppertone.

"Yeah, if you're careful. He's not going to be the ideal horse to learn on, though. He's quick and he's hair-trigger, so you might confuse him, he might dump you, but he won't buck you or anything, and he'll be better to start on than that bronc."

They walked a little ways away from the row of parked rigs to an open grassy area. Tuck turned to look back at her horse, but the mare was grazing in quick, greedy bites and didn't seem to be aware of Tuck's absence.

Mason stood at Coppertone's head and motioned Tuck toward the stirrup. "Okay now, gather up the reins in your left hand, put it on his neck there, that's it, foot in the stirrup, right hand on the cantle, no, back there, this is the cantle, this back part. Okay now, kind of spring off your right foot, there you go, don't kick him as you swing your leg over. That was fine. You settled in easy, that's good. Lots of people drop themselves like a load of bricks, and no horse likes that."

Tuck sat in that saddle, grinning like her face would

break. It felt high, but not scary. It felt good. It felt like where she'd been supposed to be, all these years.

"Okay, now what?"

"Got your foot in the other stirrup? Okay now, here's his operating instructions. Like I said, he's used to me riding him, and every shift of my weight is a cue for him to get himself under me. So try not to shift around; just sit up straight, keep your eyes forward and up, aim at looking past his ears at where you're going, so you won't slouch forward."

She got into position. It felt great.

"To get him going, just kind of gather the reins up a little, till you get a feel of his head at the other end of the reins. He's wearing a hackamore, so it's not a bit in his mouth, but it is kind of a lever action under his chin. He'll be sensitive to pressure on it, so don't pull back unless you mean him to stop, and then you better be prepared to stop, or you'll go off over his ears. So to get him going, gather up the slack, kind of lift him up with your hand, and think 'forward.' If you're thinking it, your body balance will change a little, and he'll read you."

Tuck sucked in her lip and concentrated on memorizing the instructions. This was getting complicated.

"To stop him, a quick little pressure on the reins, a little shift to the rear with your body weight, then relax your hands and legs, and think 'stop.' To turn him, think the turn like you would on a bicycle so you're leaning into it, pushing him into it with your rein hand and your inside leg. Got that?"

"No."

51

"Okay, for starters, just remember to move your rein hand the direction you want to turn, so you're laying his neck in that direction. That's all you need to know for now, just remember he's used to light cues, just a touch on the neck. Okay, take him at a walk."

Awkwardly Tuck moved her hand down the braided reins, pulling the slack through with her other hand until she felt contact, felt Coppertone lift his head as though listening for instructions. Forward, she thought, and almost involuntarily her legs tightened against the stiffness of the saddle.

/ The horse walked forward. Prepared as she was, Tuck still rocked a bit when the gentle jolts began beneath her.

"What you want," Mason called, "is controlled relaxation. Keep your body upright but your back relaxed just enough so you're moving with him, not against him."

Tuck laid the reins leftward, then right again, and Coppertone veered around a car. "Hey, it works," she yelled. For another five minutes or so she maneuvered around the grassy area at a walk, concentrating on controlled relaxation, moving with the horse, keeping upright. Then, feeling ready for more, she leaned forward a little, tightened her legs again and thought, faster.

Coppertone bounded forward into a dead gallop. Tuck was snapped backward but managed to grab the saddlehorn and pull herself upright. She hauled in on the reins and collided head-on with his neck as the horse dropped his hindquarters and plowed to a trembling stop. For an instant Tuck could see nothing but swimming redness and fireworks. When her vision cleared Mason was loping toward her. Cautiously she eased Coppertone forward into a walk again, so as not to be caught looking as dazed as she felt.

"You okay?" Mason said.

"Sure. Only he didn't quite read my mind right. I was thinking trot and he was reading run like hell."

4
_____

The remaining two and a half days of the McAlester rodeo
were incredibly full, exciting, wearying ones for Tuck. She
worked in the refreshment booth or peddling popcorn in
the stands, as much time as the management would give
her, and by the end of the last performance had added
twenty-two dollars to her wad, after donations to Grace for
groceries and a little to Merrill for oats.

Her mornings were devoted to the mare, whose name
was now Indigo. Tuck wanted Indigo to start her new life
as cleanly as Tuck herself was starting hers, and Blue Blazes
sounded too broncy. Whenever Mason came and offered,
she took time away from her own horse to have practice
rides on Coppertone, to help get her legs and her balance
ready for when she started riding Indigo. But all the rest of
the long morning hours, from six on, Tuck and Indigo
wandered the grassy perimeters of the rodeo grounds attached to each other by the rope and by their newborn
sense of belonging to each other.

At first Indigo had moments of being wild-eyed and

jumpy. A horse loping past, or a flock of youngsters darting out near her from behind parked trucks, would send her scooting to the end of the rope. There were times when Tuck was fleetingly afraid the mare would get away from her. But it never quite happened, and by the third day of Indigo's life on the rope, things seemed to be settling down.

On the morning of the last day B.C. followed Tuck out of the trailer after breakfast and settled himself into the lawn chair with one of his Louis L'Amour novels.

"When you going to start riding that horse, Tucker?"

She sighed and looked at the spot on Indigo's back where she ought to be sitting. "I'm working up to it, B.C. By gradual stages."

"Gradual stages ain't going to accomplish anything. Heck, she's standing quiet for you by now and letting you brush her all over without any fussing. I bet if you were to hop up on her back right now she wouldn't do a thing."

From inside the trailer came Grace's bellow, "B.C., you quit egging her on like that. You want her to get hurt? Leave her be."

Tuck stared some more at that silvery smoke-colored back, right there level with her chin. Indigo was lipping along the ground, her teeth searching for grass she hadn't already eaten off to earth-level. One ear twitched at a fly.

"Maybe she would be okay," Tuck mused. "You think I should try it?"

B.C. came to stand beside her. "Sure. Just cock up your knee, there, and I'll leg you up. She can't do any more than toss you off."

"You're real reassuring, you know that?"

Mason walked past, paused, came over to watch. So

55

did two other cowboys whom Tuck knew by sight, by now, if not by name.

"You going to ride her?" one of them asked. "Hell, I rode her at Joplin last fall. She's nothing. I could have shaved and read a book while I was doing my ride."

"That's easy for you to say," Tuck muttered. "Well, I guess since the event has already drawn an audience, I better try it anyway."

Mason said, "You want me to top her off for you first?"

She shook her head. "No. She knows me by now. You'd be too much like a bronc rider. She'd probably be more likely to buck with you than with me."

"Don't you *want* her to buck?" said one of the others, amazed. "Hell, that ain't going to be any fun." But he stayed to watch anyway.

Tuck hauled in her breath, grabbed a fistful of mane, and offered her knee to B.C. As she rose into the air, Indigo's head snapped up. Black jaws stopped chewing. An eye widened to a white rim.

Before Tuck was fully astride the mare was in the air and so was Tuck. Ground came up and smacked her in the face. As Tuck landed she rolled, fearful of the hooves.

"Whoopee!"

"Ride 'em Tucker!"

Nobody helped her up, but at least Mason and B.C. grabbed Indigo's rope and held the mare out of the way as Tuck climbed to her feet. The other two members of the audience sauntered away, still laughing. One said, "Hey, remember that time in Sioux Falls. . . ."

Grace slammed out of the trailer. "You fellers don't

56

have the sense God gave a goat. I told you you were going to get her hurt, and you went and done it anyway. I ought to crack your heads together."

"I'm not hurt." Tuck shook out her arms and legs to be sure she was telling the truth. Bone-wise she wasn't hurt, but she couldn't help staring a little sadly at Indigo and wishing her horse had trusted her more. She'd have liked it to be the way it was in books, instant love and understanding between horse and person.

B.C. held out his cupped hands again for her knee, but she shook her head. "Wouldn't do any good, B.C. She'd just jump out from under me again. I'm not a good enough rider yet to stick with her, especially bareback, and I don't want her to get in the habit of feeling like she's got to buck me off every time I try it. Heck, she's only doing what she was trained to do, I guess." That thought made her feel better.

Mason said, "Why don't I go get my saddle? We could try that."

They tried it. Indigo told them as plain as she could that she knew what the saddle meant, and she was ready to come out of the chute bucking, even with no chute.

Both Mason and Tuck shook their heads at the mare's snorting and plunging. "Nope. That's not going to feed the bulldog," Mason said as he pulled the saddle off again. "Tell you what. Let's get one of the bronc riders to give us a hand. That's their business, staying on a bucking horse. We'll get Jack or Dacy or one of those guys to ride her down to a walk for you, and then you can take it from there."

But Tuck shook her head. "She's my horse, Mason. Listen, I don't expect you to understand. You probably had horses all your life, as soon as you started wanting one. Well, I've been building up for this ever since I was old enough to know what a horse was. She may be just a dink of a washed-out bronc to you and the other guys, but . . . ," she hesitated, then felt her way through the words, "she's family to me. I traded the only thing I had of my real family to get her, and I just have this strong feeling that from now on, well, it's the two of us against the world. I can't explain it."

"You just did."

B.C. and Grace retired to lawn chairs on the shady side of the trailer. Tuck untied Indigo's rope from the tree and started off in search of fresh grazing, hoping Mason would come too. He did.

"So anyway," she went on, "I don't just feel like I want a bronc rider breaking her for me, even though that does seem like the logical way to do it. I'd thought about that, too, before you said it. I reckon what I want is for her to trust me so much she'll let me do whatever I want with her, and having someone else ride her down first would take that away, if you follow me."

"Sure."

Under a tree where Indigo hadn't yet grazed the area bare, they stopped and sat, Tuck holding the rope loosely, her arms propped across her knees.

Mason said, "You were wrong about me, though, what you said back there."

"What?"

"I didn't have a horse all my life. Not till I was thirteen."

She snorted. "Still. Thirteen. I bet your folks bought you a horse about the first time you asked for one, though, didn't they?"

He dropped his eyes to the ground. "I guess."

"And I suppose they come and cheer you on when you're rodeoing. I expect they bought you your truck and trailer and all that. Not to mention that expensive roping horse."

"Yeah. They did." He spoke more quietly than Tuck was ready for. "They bought me Coppertone when I was doing high school rodeo. They wanted to be able to brag about their son the National Champion High School Rodeo calf roper."

"Were you?"

"No. But close enough. I did pretty well after I got Tone. And I worked my butt off getting there, and I half hated my dad for always pushing me, always telling me afterwards what I did wrong."

"Was he a calf roper too?"

Mason laughed an unfunny laugh. "He was a corporation lawyer. Is. Never been closer to a horse than just writing out the checks to pay the bills. But he got some kind of high out of me doing it. So then I went off to college on a rodeo scholarship—"

"You mean they've got those? Like a football scholarship or some regular sport like that? I never knew that."

"Yeah. Intercollegiate rodeo is big stuff in some of these schools, Cal Poly, Texas A & M, lots of them. That's

59

when my dad bought me the truck and trailer, so I could get around the college rodeo circuit in style and reflect well on the family name."

"You sound like all is not roses between you and him now."

"All is not roses or horse manure or anything else between him and me. See, what happened was after I got out from under his thumb and started rodeoing with the college team I got to liking it. I mean, really loving it. I'd always had a love for it, I guess, but while my dad was shoving it down my throat I was gagging on it a lot. You know? But it was different in college. And then last year, halfway through my junior year, I got to realizing that I had no desire to get my law degree and go to work for him and marry some fluff-head and settle down in Wildorado for the rest of my life. I wanted to rodeo, and I figured I was good enough to make a living at it on the PRCA circuits. So I quit school, loaded up Coppertone, and lit out. And ever since then I have no father. He informs me of that fact regularly."

Tuck's jaw dropped. "But he was so *behind* you before."

"Oh, yeah. When it was a sport. But a professional rodeo cowboy just doesn't make as good bragging material as a lawyer son. He thinks I'm a bum. He's probably right," he added on a cheerier note.

Tuck thought about it all, then slapped her knee and said, "Well. I'm glad you told me about it. I like you better now. I'd just figured you for a rich guy, figured you were too young to have earned enough to buy all that expensive stuff. Heck, you're just like me in a way, except

60

you're getting into the profession with a few more things going for you. Experience. Your own rig. A good horse. . . ."

She stared thoughtfully at Indigo.

After a long quiet spell Mason said, "What *are* you aiming toward with that horse? I mean, I'll be glad to haul her for you, as long as we're both going the same direction. But let's face it, she's kind of a luxury item for somebody in your income bracket. And feeling like you do about her you're probably not aiming to just retrain her and sell her as a pleasure horse, are you?"

Tuck shook her head. "The only thing I can think of is to try to make a barrel horse out of her, since that's the only event I could ever compete in, to try to earn prize money. But against all those fancy-bred quarter horses, doesn't seem too likely she'll ever be that good even if I can get started riding her. So I don't know. I'm probably just crazy."

"I expect." He said it like crazy was one of the requirements for joining the club. Probably is, Tuck thought.

The next morning the rodeo moved out, bound westward across Oklahoma for Lawton. The moving out didn't start till nearly noon though, since almost everyone except the Olmsteads and Tuck and a few others had partied most of the night from one bar to another and were in no fit shape to travel early.

With considerable misgivings Tuck led Indigo toward Mason's horse trailer when the time came. But the mare was familiar with traveling even though an individual stall with leatherette padding wasn't her usual style, and she knew Coppertone by now. With only minimal head jerking and eye-rolling she planted one big, broken-edged hoof on the trailer floor, then the next, then heaved herself on in.

Tuck would have liked to ride with Mason, to be close to her horse and possibly for other reasons which she wasn't about to explore. But for fear of hurting Grace's and B.C.'s feelings she didn't. And besides, Mason didn't offer.

They rolled away out the gate and onto the highway, an informal caravan of friends wanting to keep in sight of one another in case Jack's trailer hitch gave out again, or Jona got into mechanical difficulties. Or just because it was nicer to get on down the road with people you know in front and behind. Tuck took a fast look back as they pulled out of the rodeo grounds and felt more of a home-pull than she had a week ago when she left 1534 Panama Street, and she'd been there three years.

Riding along with her arm out the window and her eyes on Indigo's rump up ahead, Tuck was hit with a new worry. "Hey, B.C., what's this new place going to be like? Will there be grazing for Indigo? If I have to start buying hay for her . . ."

"No problem. It's a big fairgrounds. You shouldn't have any trouble about grass, even this early in the year."

"What about in the middle of summer, when the grass dries up?"

Grace said, "We'll be up in Wyoming, Montana, the Dakotas, that time of year. There'll be grass."

"Think I'll still be riding with you then? Think you'll get sick of having me underfoot?" She tried to make it sound like she was kidding.

They laughed and kidded her back, and she relaxed. She might be hanging on by her fingernails, but at least she was a whale of a lot farther into this business than she'd expected to be so soon. And she'd signed on knowing security wasn't a big part of any rodeo person's life. She squinted into the blast of air coming in the window and began to hum.

The Lawton rodeo was a five-day affair beginning two days after the arrival of the caravan of cowboys. During those two days Tuck looked up the arena manager and got hired on as a ticket seller for the whole five days. It would only be a few hours in the early afternoon, another couple of hours early evenings, and it paid a little better than her last career although there were, of course, no meals included.

Five days at fifteen dollars a day, minus a week's worth of meal-money, and added to what she already had stashed, would put her up to the two hundred mark. She rejoiced. Well, take off for contributing to B.C.'s truck gas and a used bridle if she could ever find one. Still, it was getting up there. Five hundred by the end of six months didn't seem impossible at all, she decided.

The two vacation days before the start of the rodeo were a feast of Indigo-time for Tuck. While the mare grazed in one circle after another around the fairgrounds buildings, Tuck stood beside her, always talking, petting, brushing, and more pointedly leaning her arm across the mare's back.

At first, back pressure brought Indigo's head up and halted her jaws in their chewing. But gradually the mare

63

grew bored with it and kept her attention on her grass, even when Tuck's arm encircled her barrel like a rider's leg and the girl's ribs made a definite weight on Indigo's.

／Late on the second afternoon Tuck put her hands on the mare's back and made as easy a jump upward as she could. Indigo sidestepped and Tuck landed on her feet without having gotten where she wanted to get, but at least Indigo's reaction seemed milder than it had been before. Again Tuck jumped and again Indigo sidestepped, but this time she carried Tuck with her for maybe half a minute before Tuck lost her balance on her stiffened arms and had to come down.

A third try. Indigo danced sideways but then stood tensed and waiting to see what was up.

"That's my girl. Easy does it. Nothing to worry about, it's just me. Easy, girl. Just me up here."

By fractions of inches Tuck lowered herself until she was lying crossways on the mare's back, her elbows up like grasshopper legs, her head hanging low on the offside, feet dangling off the ground. Blood rushed to her head, and her ears began to ring, but no louder than the hallelujah chorus inside Tuck when Indigo lowered her head and began to graze again.

A cowboy walked by, his arm around one of the camp-follower girls. "Hey, Tucker, that the latest style in bronc riding? I reckon I'll have to try that next time I'm up."

Tuck raised her head high enough to see who it was. "I'm practicing up to be a trick rider. Hey, Jack, you know where I could get me an old bridle or hackamore, cheap?"

"No, but I'll put the word out. Somebody's probably got one."

64

Tuck hung across Indigo as long as she could, but it was a hard position to breathe in and every time the mare took a step, grazing, Tuck teetered. She came down, waited a few minutes until her insides all got back down to where they should be, then she tried again. Indigo moved sideways away from the initial jump, but quieted almost immediately.

Tuck was way late getting back to the trailer for supper, not wanting to stop hanging across Indigo until she was sure the lesson was well learned. When she got to the trailer she found that it had been unhitched and left standing there truckless. Inside on the table was a note.

"Gone to town for groceries. May stop off for a drink somewhere, so don't worry if we're late getting back. Your supper's on the stove. We'll bring some ice cream back."

Tuck felt mildly deserted as she lit the fire under the skillet of corned beef hash, but she told herself Grace and B.C. probably needed some time away from her. Looking at the situation from their viewpoint she could see that. From her viewpoint things were still a little lonesome though, so when supper was done and washed up after, she started out to make the rounds of the camp looking for a bridle. The knowledge that Indigo had held Tuck's weight on her back without bucking and that a bridle was now necessary for the next part of her training made a warm spot in Tuck's mood and helped burn off the chill of desertion.

At Jona's rig everything was so spiffy that Tuck didn't dare go close. The gleaming chestnut barrel racer dozed in a portable pipe-fence corral at the side of the horse trailer. Near the pickup camper Jona and her parents sat around a folding picnic table, while a charcoal fire that smelled of steak drippings slowly died out into fragrant smoke.

Tuck knew Jona would have nothing so tacky as a cheap old used bridle in her possession.

At Mason's rig there was another blast of nobody home. Coppertone was secured inside the trailer for the night, and Mason's truck, like B.C.'s, was unhitched and gone to town. Getting drunk in bars and picking up beautiful women, Tuck assumed.

It was a diamond-starred night, crisp and charged with potential excitement, something that might happen, someone who might materialize out of the dark and invite Tuck into a circle of warmth and friendliness. But the excitement was understrung with the knowledge that things like that didn't happen to Annie Tucker.

She slitted her eyes almost closed as she walked among the rigs, to better hear the night sounds: the stamping and lowing of cattle in their distant pens, guitar music, radio music, a squeaking saddle somewhere off to the right, and beneath it all the almost inaudible background weave of voices, occasionally punctured by a hoot of laughter.

There was a group that looked approachable. Four cowboys, a couple of women in jeans and boots, all sitting around the remains of a little stick fire, some on folding chairs, some hunkered down on haunches, one girl sitting on the fender of the truck.

One cowboy was saying, ". . . ugliest woman God ever strung a gut through. If I'm lyin' I'm dyin', boys, this one would've curdled your Coors. Had a can of Skoal in her back pocket."

"I think I know that one."

66

"I think I was married to that one."

Laughter. Tuck laughed with them, not so loud as to draw attention though, and sidled up to lean against the back wheel well of the truck.

"No, now, let me finish my story. Hey there, Tuck, how you doin'? Well anyhow, there I was stranded in Nowata, and you haven't been *stranded* till you've been stranded in Nowata; no fuel pump, no mechanics till Monday morning, and here she is offering me her motel room. I've got maybe a dollar ninety-eight in my jeans, no credit cards, no nothing. . . ."

He glanced at Tuck. She could feel him weighing the propriety of continuing his story with her listening in.

She pushed her lips into a smile. "Well, see y'all."

"See ya," they chorused after her.

But Indigo watched Tuck's approach as though she might have been aware of the girl's absence, and she stood placidly listening to Tuck's voice talking soft nonsense, and that helped.

It was the middle of the night when Grace and B.C. came in, turning on lights and rattling grocery bags and rousing Tuck from her nap on their bed, since they were driving hers.

"Wake up, honey," Grace bellowed. "We got rocky road and we got chocolate marshmallow ripple. Course it's all kindie melted by now, but we'll have a dish anyway. What's your pleasure?"

"That chocolate whatever-you-said." Tuck was still fuzzy-minded from sleep. "What time is it, anyhow?"

"Quarter of two," B.C. said as he reached around Grace's stubby figure to get into the dish cupboard. "We stopped off at this little place that had a western band, and Grace got to dancing. Didn't think I was ever going to get her off that dance floor. She gets to dancing and there's no stopping her. Won't quit till she's had a romp with every man in the place."

Grace sighed as she scooped out the softened blobs of ice cream. "Well, what can I do? I'm too tenderhearted to turn any of them boys down. I tell you, honey, it's hell being a sex symbol."

By the time Tuck had bellied up to the table and wakened her mind with chocolate marshmallow ripple, the shadows of her earlier mood had burned off like morning fog in the sunrise.

"Hey. Almost forgot." B.C. reached around to one of the grocery bags and pulled out a fistful of leather. "I picked this up for you, if you want it. It was only five bucks, thought you might could use it on your mare."

Tuck accepted the hackamore with delighted wonder. It was old and beat-up looking, but the bosal and reins were braided rawhide just like Mason's, and beat-up or not it was exactly what Tuck had been looking for. She fished out the five dollar bill with hardly a twinge.

She glanced up at B.C. suddenly and said, "They sell hackamores in the Supervalue around here? That must be some town."

He laughed. "Naw, cowboy at the bar where we were had it. Any time those boys run out of cash before they run out of drinking capacity, they're likely to sell most anything they got; their grandmothers, trophy buckles, oh, no offense, Tuck."

Grace waved her spoon at him. "That's all right," she

68

said stoutly, "Tuck didn't sell her buckle for anything frivolous. She was saving a friend from a one-way trip to the packing plant. You'd've done the same thing and you know it, you old buzzard."

Tuck leaned back in the booth, laced her fingers across her stomach, and watched the two of them with a glow on her face.

5

Tuck was up early the next morning, wakened by her eagerness to try the hackamore on Indigo. But the trailer had such stillness coming from it that she knew Grace and B.C. were a long way from ready for breakfast.

"Mornin', old darling," she said softly to the mare, who was still curled up on the ground like a dog in her sleeping position. Indigo heaved herself to her feet, yawned hugely, stretched fore and aft, then shook herself and sent dust and grass bits into the air. She stood quietly through the morning brushing but stiffened her ears as the new hackamore appeared at the end of her nose.

"It's just another halter. Except when you've got it on you'll have to do everything I want you to. You're going to learn to stop and go and turn and not buck. Got that? If you buck while you're wearing this, your ears and tail are going to fall off, and your mane's going to turn to snakes. And your belly button will come unscrewed. What? You don't believe me? Did I ever lie to you? Come on, let's try it on."

Cautiously she unbuckled the nylon halter, slipped it

down as she'd seen Mason do, then rebuckled it around her horse's neck but free of her head. Slowly she slipped the hackamore home. Indigo accepted it uneasily but without a fight. She tried to lower her head to graze and was startled to feel the bosal tighten around her face.

\"No, no grazing. The hackamore means work time."

Tuck slipped the reins over Indigo's head and began to walk, keeping her hand tight on the reins just under the hackamore's lever, which tightened beneath the horse's jaw when the reins were pulled.

"Whoa. Good girl!" They stopped, started again, and repeated the stops and starts all around the fairgrounds buildings until Indigo began to respond on her own to the whoa command and the reins. Finally they stopped near yesterday's tree, and Tuck allowed the mare to drop her head to the grass.

"Now's the time," she thought. "It's not going to get any easier if I put it off."

She began by jumping up easy, getting her weight up onto her arms, on Indigo's back. The mare sidestepped. Tuck tried again. On her third try she made it into dead man's position, draped over Indigo's back while the mare resumed grazing.

Cautiously Tuck stiffened her arms, shifted counter-clockwise, lifted her right knee . . . the leg was over Indigo's croup. She was astride!

Indigo's head came up. The jaws stopped chewing while ears and eyes pivoted backward to see what was going on back there. Tuck crooned and voice-caressed for all she was worth.

After an eternity, when Tuck was running out of

breath to hold, Indigo lowered her head and bit off a swatch of grass.

For a good long time Tuck sat there, just relishing being astride her horse and giving Indigo a chance to get used to the feel of her up there. But eventually it seemed time for the next step. She pulled up on the reins. Indigo's head lifted. Tuck clucked to her, and squeezed gently with her legs.

Indigo moved forward tensely, uncertain of what was expected of her.

"Good girl, that's it."

Tuck became aware of people watching, a handful of ropers out working their horses in the morning quiet time. She tried to ignore them.

Indigo stopped. Tuck urged her forward again. The mare broke into a shuffle-step that became a canter.

"Whoa. Easy, girl."

The canter became a buck, and Tuck somersaulted to the ground. Even as she landed she was already scrambling to her feet, the reins still in her hand. Indigo had broken into a nervous sweat.

Mason and Coppertone were there suddenly. "Need any help over here? Hey, you got yourself a hackamore. Looked like you were making some progress with her, up till that last little bit."

He dismounted and offered his cupped hands for Tuck's knee. She accepted before fear could take over. In one smooth movement she was in the air and settled again on Indigo's back.

They started out walking, with Mason between the two horses and leading both of them. He held Indigo's

72

hackamore by the cheek strap, to be out of the way of Tuck's rein control. They walked and walked and walked, and gradually Tuck could feel the tension going out of the spine and muscles on which she sat. Then they practiced some whoas and starts. It was hard to tell whether Indigo was obeying the rein pressure or just doing what Coppertone did, but at any rate she behaved.

Tuck said, "Why don't you try just riding beside us now?"

He mounted Coppertone and they set off, first walking, then slow-jogging, then walking again. At every turn Tuck neck-reined the mare, who would have turned in any case just to be following the lead of the other horse.

Eventually they had to stop. Mason needed to give Coppertone his morning workout, Tuck needed to get ready for her ticket-selling job, and Indigo needed to stop learning for the day before she got tired and cranky. Tuck and Mason ended the ride back at the home trailer, where B.C. and Grace gave them applause and whoops of congratulations.

Tuck dismounted, sweaty and horsehairy and grinning so hard her face ached. The joy in her was like helium, threatening to float her clear off the ground if she didn't grab somebody and hug. Grace got it, and so did B.C. Mason was already gone, but he would have been too scary to hug anyhow.

The afternoon program, that first day, was scheduled to start at two o'clock. At one Tuck reported to the little tollbooth building at the fairgrounds' main entrance, where the man in charge of ticket sales gave her her instructions. Two dollars each for adults, green tickets. A

73

buck apiece for kids twelve to eighteen, tan tickets, don't argue about ages unless it's obvious they're trying to pull one over on you. Kids under twelve free. She was given a short, pocketed apron with change, tickets, and programs worth two dollars each.

As the cars began to roll in, Tuck learned to work down the line, selling the tickets as quickly as possible so as to get the cars through the gate with minimum delay. It was fun. Easier than selling food, and almost everyone coming in was in a jovial mood. She found herself welcoming people as though they were guests in her home, and she loved the feeling.

There were no tips though, and by three-thirty business had dropped off so much she was excused and told to come back about six for the evening crowd. Two and a half hours of work. Seven-fifty added to her bankroll. As she walked toward the stands she sucked air in through her teeth and pondered her precarious fortune. At the rate the money was coming in it was going to be one tight squeak, getting five hundred ahead in six months, and that was not counting unexpected expenses, like if Indigo got sick or needed shoes.

She wandered to the area along the arena fence, near the chutes, and found a place to stand where she could see but not be in anybody's way. Saddle broncs were on. As she watched, she tried to put herself in the horses' minds, to understand what it had been like for Indigo. She watched a big pinto being hazed into his chute from the stock pens. That was Upset; she knew some of their names by now. A cowboy she didn't recognize, who had drawn Upset in yesterday's drawing, climbed to the top of the chute with his association saddle on his hip and dropped the saddle onto Upset's back. It was a strange-looking saddle, high backed and hornless with slim U-shaped stirrups designed to release the rider's foot in a fall. Another cowboy reached under Upset's belly with a long hook and snagged the front and back cinches, and with a practiced motion drew them tight.

The eight-second horn sounded for the rider in the arena. Tuck glanced in and saw B.C. cavorting along the fence, making faces at the children in the stands. He wore huge patched cut-off jeans held up by orange suspenders. Under the jeans were red tights that looked like long underwear. He wore baseball shoes for maximum traction when the bulls came after him and a straw hat with bobbing flowers.

There was no real work for him to do during saddle bronc, Tuck knew, but he loved being in the arena anyhow.

The announcer said, "Our next rider up is a young fellow name of Ted Diaz from Plano, Texas. Us old-timers remember his dad, Jim Diaz, one of the best bronc riders in the business. Let's give him a welcome, he's on a horse called Upset, who was a National Finals saddle bronc two years running."

In the chute, Diaz lowered himself carefully into the saddle and wrapped twice around his hand the thick braided rope attached to Upset's broad bronc halter. Tuck made a mental note not ever to try riding Indigo with a halter and lead rope, for fear it would remind her of her bronc days.

Diaz nodded to the man who worked the chute gate.

As the gate swung out, the saddling helper gave a jerk to the flank strap around Upset's belly. The pinto leaped. Diaz's heels arced up across the horse's shoulders in the sweeping, spurring motion necessary for a qualifying ride. Upset flung himself high, swapped ends, came down in a jarring series of buck-jumps, twists, plunges. The crowd roared. It was better bucking than Indigo ever thought of doing, Tuck realized, and furthermore she got the feeling that the horse was enjoying every second of it.

When the buzzer sounded, Diaz let go and sailed through the air like he was sitting on an invisible rocking chair. He landed on his feet, bowed to the crowd, then modestly fetched his hat from the dust, brushed it off against his seat, and bowlegged it out of the ring.

Tuck climbed up into the stands and found a shady seat on an uncrowded bench. After a few more broncs the ring was cleared and the barrels were rolled in for barrel racing. While the barrels were being set in place at measured distances, B.C. left the ring and came back in again in what appeared to be a tiny cart pulled by a harnessed chicken. It was fake, of course. She'd watched him assembling the whole thing back at the trailer. The cart was plywood that came apart for flat storage, and it hung around B.C.'s body by a harness arrangement, and the chicken was rubber. But it was surprisingly convincing even so, and she loved it.

As the first barrel racer galloped in, Tuck leaned forward and studied every move that horse and rider made. Or tried to. Eighteen seconds wasn't much studying time. She felt the ride in her own body as she maneuvered Indigo through the cloverleaf pattern, dashing home in

76

record-breaking time. Ah, daydreams. She laughed at herself, but she didn't quite dismiss the possibility, either. Just because there was no reason to think Indigo had the makings of a top barrel horse, there was also no reason to think she didn't. Worth a try, for sure, Tuck thought, especially since it seemed to be the only way a girl could earn more than just little dibs and dabs of money, rodeoing.

And the dreams were there in Tuck's head. The big dreams. Her own rig. Her own home on wheels, a pickup camper like Mason's and Jona's with a soft bed, and her own bathroom even if it was only two feet square, and Indigo's trailer on behind with a portable corral like Jona's so Indigo wouldn't have to spend her whole life tied up to something. But before she could even start working on that dream, there was the buckle to get out of hock.

Why wasn't I born rich instead of merely beautiful? she thought.

Tuck and Grace ate an easy cold supper of baloney sandwiches. B.C. couldn't eat with his makeup on, so he usually dined on a malt with a straw from the concession stand on show days. Then Tuck brought Indigo her night bucket of water and left to do her ticket selling.

She got through in time to watch the last of the team roping. Mason and Jack were up, Mason heading, Jack heeling. The steer came barreling out of his chute, Mason and Jack on his left and right about two leaps behind. Coppertone flattened himself for the run and got himself positioned just right, behind and beside the fleeing steer. Mason's rope settled around the horns. Coppertone braked and hauled beef backward as Mason did a lightning-fast dally around the saddlehorn, avoiding the loss of his fingers by a fraction as the rope jerked taut. Already Jack's loop was under the steer's belly like the jaws of a trap. Hind feet stepped into the loop, Jack jerked and dallied, and instantly the three animals froze in a taut line, the two horses facing each other, steer strung out in between.

The arena judge dropped his flag and the time went up. Nineteen point four two three seconds. Applause. Good enough to be in the money, Tuck figured. But she knew team roping purses had to be divided between the two ropers, and day money wasn't going to cover the two new tires Mason was needing. She hoped he'd won a go-round in calf roping or steer wrestling, one or the other, today.

After team roping came the grand finale event of the rodeo. Bull riding. Tuck shivered in anticipation of the sheer evil power of the bulls. Broncs were content to unload their riders, she thought, and even make a game out of it like Upset did. But the bulls—they wanted to kill.

Now B.C.'s real work began.

The first bull was a gray part-Brahman with black spots on his head and shoulders. Orient Express. He came tornadoing out and, just clear of the chute, began a clockwise spin, trying to drop his rider into the well, the center of the spin, where he could gore the man to a bloody pulp. B.C. danced near the bull's head, waving his arms, thumbing his nose, turning to flip his bottom up invitingly in front of the bull's horns. Orient Express was distracted long enough to break his spin and go off in another direction. Just as the horn sounded, the rider came off.

B.C. romped in front of the bull, taunting him. The bull gave chase. B.C. lit out for the fence and leaped high, clawing up the mesh fencing just as the bull's horns swept in an angry arc below B.C.'s baggy cut-offs.

The bull turned and trotted away, dropping off the bull rope as he went. The weight of the cowbell that had dangled from the underside of the rope throughout the ride pulled the whole contraption off. Grace had explained the workings of the bull rope to Tuck, told her there'd be no way of getting the rope, which was the rider's only handhold, off of an angry bull after a ride. No safe way, anyhow.

There was a slight delay while the second bull raised a ruckus in the chute.

B.C. called to the announcer in a loud stage voice, "I used to be a bull rider."

"You used to be a bull rider?" came the announcer's reply. "Why'd you give it up?"

"Had to."

"You had to? How's come?"

"Doctor's order."

"You say your doctor ordered you to give it up? Why?"

"I had a stomach condition."

"What stomach condition did you have?"

"No guts."

The crowd laughed and Tuck laughed with them, just out of feeling good.

"All right now, folks, I believe we're about ready to go with our second rider for the evening. This is Jack Berry from up Vermillion, South Dakota way, and he's drawn one of the rankest bulls we've ever seen on the pro rodeo circuit. Folks, this bull is named Hellbender, and that's not one bit of an overstatement. He's only been rode once that I know of, and he's put a whole passel of doctors' kids through school, all the busted-up cowboys he's got to his credit. Let's give old Jack a hand, here."

The applause started, then died as the bull crashed through the opening chute gate. He bucked high and dirty, fishtailing in mid-leap, lashing his mammoth body sideways both ways at once. On his first jarring landing, Jack was knocked back on the bull's back, a hopeless position. One more twisting plunge and Jack was off.

But not off! Instead of falling clean, the man's body was swung around his grip hand, twisting the hand inside the rawhide grip. Jack was flung across the bull's back. He dangled and flapped like a rag doll, his caught arm up around his head.

The crowd sucked in its collective breath. One or two soft screams pierced the night.

B.C. darted in beside the maddened bull. He made a desperate grab for the cowboy's rope end, bobbing just out of reach over the bull's shoulders. Hellbender swung his head around and, bellowing his hatred, embedded his horn in the small of B.C.'s back.

Men from the sidelines converged on the bull, but no one could get close. B.C. stumbled, made one last grab for the rope. Missed. Fell. Tried to get up but the bull was on him. In that instant Jack twisted around and got his free hand up to the rope and jerked it loose. He fell on top of B.C.

Tuck couldn't look. Couldn't look away either. A flag-waving judge caught Hellbender's attention just long enough for three other men to jump into the mess and drag B.C. and Jack out of the arena.

Tuck was already on her feet, running, stumbling down the grandstand steps. Even so, the ambulance doors were swinging shut as she got there.

"B.C.," she yelled, hitting her fists on the ambulance.

"You family?" a white-coated attendant asked her.

"Yes. Where are you taking him? How bad is he?"

"St. Luke's hospital, ma'am. Fourth Avenue and Grover. We want to get him there as quick as possible. Don't know how bad he is. You got a car?"

"Yes. We'll be there. Hurry."

On her way to the trailer she collided with Grace, who was running, white-faced, toward the ambulance. Tuck turned her around and together they bolted for the truck. Fumbling, crying, Grace unhitched the trailer so they could drive faster, and the two of them flung themselves into the truck.

All the way to town Grace said things like, "It's probably not all that bad. Rodeoers get busted up all the time. They don't think anything about it. They're tough roosters or they wouldn't be doing rodeo, and B.C.'s as tough as the rest of them. He's tangled with bulls before and always come out of it just fine."

But neither of them believed it.

A broken rib, lots of muscle damage, a torn mouth where apparently a hoof had landed. Internal organs miraculously missed by the horn that went most of the way through B.C., back to front. Jack Berry walked out of the hospital with a sprained wrist and a shoulder full of separated muscles and torn ligaments.

It was the middle of the night before the doctor came

81

to Grace and Tuck in the waiting room on the surgery floor. The room was littered with cowboys, men to whom hospitals were a part of life and who wore their casts and slings almost as nonchalantly as their Justins. There were card games going on in two corners, and long booted legs sprawling across the floor, and a general air of being there because it was more fun than being in a bar, not because they were worried about the ability of B.C. or Jack to withstand a little bull-play.

But they were there.

/ Tuck watched them during the long wait and loved them all, even the ones she didn't know from Adam's off ox.

Grace took center stage and stood for the doctor's report. Tuck stood behind her and propped her up by the shoulders until they both understood that the news was good.

"How soon can he get out of here?" Grace asked.

The doctor frowned. "I'd prefer to keep him at least a week, but I've had dealings with you rodeo people before, and your recuperative powers never cease to amaze me."

"What does that mean?" Grace demanded.

"It means that I will allow you to take him home in two to three days, depending on how he comes along, *but*. He's got to have complete bed rest. He's going to be sick and sore for a long time, Mrs. Olmstead, and he mustn't use those back muscles at all. Can you keep him in bed?"

Tuck's eyes widened. She tuned out the rest of the medical talk as the impact of it all finally hit her. B.C. and Grace would have to go home.

I don't even know where they live, she thought

frantically. Or even if they've *got* a home somewhere. But what am I going to do then? And what about Indigo? I won't have anywhere to live if I stay with the rodeo. And if I go home with them, which they might not even want me to for all I know, I wouldn't have any way of getting Indigo there, and maybe no place to keep her when we got there. Oh, damn! Just when everything was getting so good.

6

For the next two days Tuck put off making the decision because it wasn't yet forced on her. It made her days heavy and her nights restless, but she wasn't willing to commit herself to either of the no-win directions until she had to.

In the mornings she rode Indigo. They went slowly, uneasily, and sometimes Tuck fell off because her grip and balance weren't developed enough yet to stick with sudden movements, like when a motorcycle spooked Indigo. And once Indigo got upset because she didn't understand the neckreining; Tuck was pushing too hard, trying to get her around a corner, and the mare simply dropped her head and bucked the girl off. But things got better between them gradually. If it hadn't been for the end of the week looming up at Tuck she'd have been happy to the point of pain those mornings.

Afternoons and evenings she alternated between ticket-selling, trips to the hospital with Grace, and just staring moodily around her, not knowing how she could stay here without Grace and B.C. nor how she could bring herself to leave it.

She did ponder the possibilities of moving in with someone else, even went so far as to walk slowly through the welter of pickup campers, vans, and battered motor homes that comprised the traveling town, trying to catalog who lived in each one and if there were any possible openings. She didn't yet know all of the regulars, but still it seemed to her that in this overwhelmingly male community there just was no place for a stray of the female variety. Most of the rigs seemed to house from one to four cowboys. A few had husband-wife teams where the wives rode barrels. There was one camper that appeared to house two barrel girls, and there was Jona who lived alone but in such a state of tidyness and parental company that Tuck couldn't conceive of trying to inflict herself on Jona's life.

It occurred to her as a passing thought that if Mason would marry her that would solve all her problems, but she figured just asking him to haul her horse was about all the favor she could expect from anybody.

Then it occurred to her that maybe he'd take her along without the marriage part, but she knew better than to suggest that. So instead of suggesting anything, she just laid her problem out in front of him.

He shook his head. "I know about everybody that follows these rodeos, and I can't think of anybody but Olmsteads that you'd be safe with. You really hit it lucky, hooking up with them. Oh, there's some cowboys that would probably take you along with them for a while, but they'd only have one purpose in mind, and you don't want that."

"No."

He thought some more. "Where is it Grace and B.C.

live, anyway? They've told me, but I forgot. Somewhere around northern Oklahoma, isn't it? Southern Kansas?"

"Blackwell, Oklahoma." Tuck had found out that much.

"Blackwell. Blackwell. Hmmm. Well, if you decide to go back home with them I could probably haul Indigo up there for you after this rodeo is over. There's a week between it and the next one."

Tuck thanked him and wandered on, half relieved that at least there was one workable solution and half depressed because that solution was pulling her away from the rodeo. She dragged her toes through the dust walking back toward home in the suddenly chilly twilight. She was through work for the day but wasn't in the mood to watch the action in the arena.

Another depressing thought assailed her. Grace hadn't yet actually invited her to come home with them. The subject had been shied around by both of them, these past days. And what if they lived someplace where she couldn't keep a horse? On the other hand, what if they lived someplace where she could get a job and be earning her five hundred while B.C. was recuperating? She walked faster.

Grace was standing beside the truck watching for Tuck. "You going in with me? Visiting hours will be half over by the time we get there if we don't get a move on."

B.C. was sitting up in his bed and smiling on the half of his face that wasn't bandaged. "Good news," he called as they came through the door. "Doc says I can leave tomorrow. You're supposed to go find him and talk to him, get all the instructions."

Grace went to find the doctor, and Tuck pulled up

86

the chair beside his bed. She felt uncomfortable in the hospital room, as though sickness might throw out a net and catch her, too.

"Well now," B.C. said in a voice that was serious, for him. "You planning on coming back to Blackwell with us, Miss Tucker?"

"I didn't know I was invited."

"Course you're *invited*. That's not the point."

"Well, it's pretty much of a point to me," she flared. "Grace never said boo about it. I didn't know whether you'd want some other person around all the time like a flea on a dog. How am I supposed to know if I'm invited or not, if nobody tells me?"

"She didn't say anything," he explained patiently, "because we both knew how much you wanted to follow the rodeos and we didn't want to make you feel like you were obliged to stick with us when you'd rather not, just because we were in a little bit of a rough time."

"You mean you *want* me to come? You need me?"

"Now you're not to worry about that. Grace and I are a couple of pretty tough old birds, and we been through worse than this in our young years. But for one thing, we like having you around. You're a nice, cheerful kid, and you laugh at my jokes, and you've got a good spirit to you, and you are our kind of people even if we haven't known you all that long. Rodeo folks are a separate breed for sure, and you're one of 'em, and we like having you around. Okay? Okay. Next thing is, from what Doc's been saying it looks like I'm going to be needing a full-time nurse for the next few months, and that's going to be more nursing than Grace has the patience for. Having another woman in the house to help out would make it an awful lot easier on her. But like I said, don't make your decision on that count."

As Tuck absorbed these new aspects, the idea of sticking with Grace and B.C. began looking better. "What about my horse? Would there be a place for her there?"

"No problem. We got a little ranch out there. Nothing fancy, but there's an old barn and plenty of pasture. She'd be welcome to it, if you can get her hauled up there."

"One other thing," Tuck said. "Would there be someplace around there where I could get a part-time job, do you think? I've only got six months to earn that five hundred dollars, you remember. To get my buckle back. And I was thinking if I came home with you maybe I'd be able to get some kind of waitress job or something. Part-time, so I could still help Grace, naturally."

B.C.'s half-face frowned. "I don't believe I'd count on that if I was you. We're away out in the country. It's possible, I suppose, but don't count on it."

By the time Grace came back Tuck had made her decision, but she didn't feel very good about it.

B.C. was released at noon the next day. With her heart feeling wrenched out of her body, Tuck said goodbye to Indigo, who would be following tomorrow after the rodeo ended, and to the rodeo itself—all the faces that were beginning to develop names, and all the sounds and smells that had become familiar and dear to her these past two weeks. Charcoal fires. Horse manure. Saddles creaking, and cowboys laughing and yelling insults to one another, and three kinds of music all going at once.

"I'll be back," she vowed to them and to herself.

Grace drove the rig as far as the hospital, then turned the driving over to Tuck so that she herself could ride in the trailer with B.C. where he could lie down on the bed.

Tuck didn't tell them she didn't have a driver's license or that she'd only driven the drivers' training car at school. She figured if she was going to be worth her keep as a helper she'd better start in now. Cautiously she eased the truck into gear and coasted out of the hospital drive, bouncing it a little when she braked for the stop sign but not doing too badly, all things considered.

The trailer bothered her, looming back there and causing a swing in the truck's rear end if she wasn't careful. It seemed to her that it took forever to get out of Lawton and onto the turnpike headed northeast toward Oklahoma City. It got better then. She began to relax and go with the feel of the truck, and only had bad moments when huge semis whooshed past her and rocked the truck and trailer in their backwash. She tensed up again in the traffic around Oklahoma City but forced herself to keep the truck down to the speed she felt comfortable with, never mind everybody else going around her.

From there on it was a clear shot north on 35, a good uncluttered highway where Tuck could relax again and sing as she rolled along. At the Blackwell exit she stopped for gas and exchanged places with Grace, who knew the way from there.

Home, when they got there, turned out to be a small square frame house whose bright pink paint had luckily lost several degrees of brightness to the sun and the dust. It sat at the end of a long rutted lane, and lane and lawn were outlined in sagging barbed wire. Guarding the house

89

were huge cottonwood trees, and behind it, partly hidden by weeds, were a few unpainted sheds and a smallish barn, all leaning to the windward.

As Tuck did a slow pivot she took in the gently rolling pastureland beyond the fence, the flat bright green wheatfields beyond the road to the west. It felt quiet out here. Private. A person could yell her loudest and not get shushed or feel silly, for fear of being heard.

She decided she liked it.

The house smelled musty and mousy from being shut up for the month that Grace and B.C. had been on the road. Starting first thing the next morning the two women aired the place out, dusted every surface, and cleaned out the places where the mice had been. B.C. was exhausted after the trip and slept all day in the little bedroom off the living room. All the rooms were small and square, with rag rugs on top of worn linoleum, and peeling veneer furniture. Downstairs were living room, bedroom, kitchen, bathroom, and junk room behind the kitchen where, by squeezing past the freezer and a stack of old feed bags and rubber boots and ropes and who knows what all else, you could get out the back door.

When the house was passable and while B.C. slept, Grace went into town for groceries, and Tuck bee-lined for the barn. By anybody else's standards it wasn't much of a barn, only about the size of a pregnant garage and smelling more like oil cans than livestock, plank floors sloping at funhouse angles and impenetrable piles of junk almost everywhere. But to Tuck it was the home of the one and only Indigo, at least for the time being, and that gave it a wash of shrine-atmosphere.

By late afternoon when Mason drove in Tuck had cleaned the barn's one big stall to the full extent that it was capable of being cleaned, bedded it with the cobwebby remains of a bale of straw she'd unearthed in the loft, and fitted it with a scrubbed and filled grain bucket. At B.C.'s instructions when he woke up from his nap, she had also hiked out across the pasture near the lane and closed a barbed wire gate separating that small pasture from a hundred-acre expanse of grassland adjoining it. He'd explained that the big pasture belonged to his brother, whose ranch bordered the little bit of land that was B.C.'s. The small pasture wouldn't be needed this early in the season, and it would be handier to have Indigo close to home in case she was hard to catch, B.C. said.

Both horses, blue roan and copper buckskin, were turned out that evening for an orgy of running and rolling and delicious freedom from the confines of life on the road. Grace, Tuck, and Mason sat on the front porch near the open window to B.C.'s bedroom and enjoyed the sight of the horses playing until it was too dark to see them anymore.

Every day the next week Tuck went out in search of gainful employment. She put on the better of her two sets of jeans and shirts and set out in the truck, following Grace's suggestions or just her own instincts. She stopped at highway cafes, even gas stations. She went all the way into Blackwell in one direction and Ponca City in the

91

other, left her name at the state employment offices there, asked door-to-door at businesses that looked like possibilities. "Sorry, hon, afraid we can't use you." The local high school kids were on waiting lists ahead of her at the fast-food places. Other businesses didn't hire anyone under eighteen, especially without a high school diploma. It was too early in the spring for the seasonal touristy businesses.

By the end of the week she had spent twenty-two precious dollars on truck gas and had not a thing to show for it except the realization that she wasn't going to earn her five hundred from here. After that depressing fact sank in, she settled into a routine of helping Grace in the mornings and working Indigo in the afternoons.

It began to look like Indigo was her only route to fortune, Indigo learning to be a barrel horse, and not just to be one but to be a good enough to earn day money when they got back on the rodeo circuit. With that goal to shoot for, Tuck dug into the training in earnest.

Hour after hour they walked, jogged, and eventually loped around and across the pasture, which was a flat open square of about five acres. Lots of times Indigo took off running when she got into the lope, and lots of times the running turned to bucking and Tuck plowed the farm with her nose. And there were times when Indigo ignored the neckreining, set her muscles against it and refused to turn, especially while she was loping. That worried Tuck, knowing how lightning-fast and tight the turns were going to have to be around barrels, racing. But Tuck went at it every day with unflagging determination anyhow.

About the middle of the third week Tuck had a talk with B.C. about her plans for Indigo. They were all eating lunch around his bed as usual, so Grace could help him. He still couldn't lift his right arm because of the torn back muscles, so meals were a community effort.

"I want to try to make a barrel horse out of her, B.C. I don't know if she's got any talent for it at all, but it's the only thing I can see to do with her, to make any money. Thing is, we need barrels to practice around, and I've got to get a saddle of some kind and get her used to wearing it, and I feel like I really need somebody who knows what they're doing to give me some pointers. So. Can you solve all my problems?"

"Now, you know me, Tucker. Anything I don't know I'll make up. The barrels shouldn't be any problem. Take the truck and go hit a few gas stations, the town dump, places like that. You want fifty-five gallon oil drums, and you ought to be able to scare up three of 'em without having to spend more than a few bucks apiece, maybe nothing.

"Saddle? Let's see. You might call over to Grover's," he said to Grace. "Seems to me I saw an old stock saddle of some kind out in his barn. He'd probably loan it to you for a while, since they sold all their horses when the kids grew up."

That was B.C.'s brother. He'd been over a few times since they got home to see B.C. and talk about the cattle they owned together. But Grace had explained to Tuck early on that relations were a little strained between the two households since Grover had divorced his good old wife after the kids got grown and moved in a loudmouth redhead half his age that he'd met in a bar in Tulsa and who was after his ranch just as sure as warts on a toad.

93

B.C. went on. "Now all you need is a local expert."

"That little Ensley girl does barrels, doesn't she?" Grace said. "That's just a couple of miles from here, close enough so you could ride over on your horse if you wanted. I expect she'd help you. What was her name again, B.C.?"

"Betty? Becky?"

"Betsy."

Tuck had her misgivings about anybody named Betsy, but she wasn't in a position to be too fussy.

Two phone calls later she had the promise of the loan of Grover's saddle and an appointment after school that afternoon with Betsy the Barrel Racer.

Lunch dishes were one of Tuck's self-appointed jobs, and she held herself to it even today, but as soon as the last spoon was shot into the silverware drawer she was off and running. It took a whole string of gas stations almost all the way to Ponca City before Tuck had her three barrels, but all of them were donated free by gas station guys who were glad to get rid of them. It gave Tuck a momentary twinge to roll the dirty, smelly things into the back of the truck, her former and future bedroom. But it was for a good cause.

On the way home she stopped at Grover's for the saddle. The redheaded woman watched from the house window but didn't come out, which was fine with Tuck who would have felt uncomfortable meeting her, knowing what she did about the woman.

The saddle Grover dragged out was the worst looking saddle Tuck had even seen. It was dusty. It had green mold growing around the metal parts. The sheepskin lining was but a memory, and the leather covering the top of the

94

horn was ripped loose and flapped like a kid's front tooth.

It was better than nothing, Tuck told herself, but she wasn't at all convinced. She thanked Grover, grabbed the saddle, and left before her acting ability ran out.

As she drove away, the truck radio said four-thirty. Time to go meet Betsy. With a whole lot less than twenty-one-gun enthusiasm she drove past the home lane and on down the dirt road the two miles Grace had told her, to the mailbox that said Ensley.

Heck, the whole place is cute, Tuck thought, disgusted. The house was Old English cottagy, with shaped and trimmed bushes, for heaven's sake. It didn't look anything like Oklahoma. Behind the house was a little Old Englishy stable, and the dog in the yard was a Pomeranian.

"And there she is," Tuck muttered. "The Betsy doll."

The kid looked maybe eleven or twelve. She had short, dark, curly hair and creased jeans and not a speck of dirt on her red gingham western shirt. The pony she was saddling at the hitch rail in front of the stable was an equally spotless black and white pinto just the right size for the munchkin.

Tuck slapped on a smile and approached. For some reason she was more intimidated by this little squirt than by anybody she could ever remember, and she didn't know why.

"Hi. I'm Tuck Tucker. I called and talked to your mom?"

"Hi." Betsy had to look way up to hit Tuck's eye level. "Mom said you wanted to learn about barrel racing. I thought maybe you'd bring your horse, but that's okay. You can watch me and Buttons. This is Buttons."

95

"Naturally," Tuck muttered.

"Come on, the course is over here. Have you been riding a long time?"

" 'Bout a month."

Betsy tried not to look startled.

"What kind of horse do you have? Is it a trained barrel horse?"

"Saddle bronc that washed out of rodeo work. I've been riding her about a month. She doesn't buck too much anymore."

Betsy absorbed this in tactful silence.

They entered an arena enclosed with split rail landscape fencing. The barrels were painted red and appeared never to have been rained on or mud-splattered. Betsy pointed out two poles stuck in the ground about twelve feet apart, a short distance inside the arena.

"Between those poles is my pretend starting line. I time myself from there. Here. You could time me if you want. It's kind of hard to do while you're riding." She handed Tuck a stopwatch from her shirt pocket, then mounted. Her saddle was a streamlined black job with a red padded seat. Tuck avoided the thought of the saddle that lay in her truck.

"First I have to warm him up," Betsy said. "I'll go back out of the arena for that, so he knows that any time he's in here it's serious business. You don't ever want to work your horse fast until you've warmed him up, or he can pull a muscle."

As she rode away, Tuck thought, It's not going to be easy, taking lessons from this sawed-off smart-alec.

Betsy and Buttons cantered up and down the dirt

road for several minutes, then did some circles in front of the stables, both directions. Finally they came back into the arena. "Okay now, hit the stem on the watch just as his head passes the posts and again when he comes back through the posts. Here we go."

⌐ She turned the pony away from the barrels, kicked him into a nervous leap, brought him up short, then, when his excitement reached a near frenzy, she spun him around shot him across the arena toward the right barrel. Tuck was so fascinated by the show she almost forgot to hit the watch stem. The pony churned dirt going around the first barrel, dug in and bolted toward the second, but cut it too close and knocked it to the ground. He leaped for the third, got around it in good shape, then tore for home, and throughout the entire run Besty yipped and yowled like nothing human. On the stretch run she flailed Buttons with the rein ends and booted him in the flanks with feet out of the stirrups.

When Betsy slid to the ground and came back to Tuck for her time score, she was flushed and sweated and powdered with dust, and just a whole lot more likeable than she'd been twenty-two seconds before.

7

It was too dark to ride by the time Tuck got home, ate the supper that was waiting, and helped B.C. with his eating while Grace got the dishes underway. There was enough moonlight, though, to roll the barrels out of the truck and into place in the pasture, and that gave Tuck considerable satisfaction. She itched to get the saddle on Indigo, if only to see how it looked, but figured it might be smarter to wait till daylight in case there was a battle.

She brushed the barrel-rust off her palms and went inside, hating to leave the crisp night air but wanting company. Grace was in B.C.'s room, where the television and two comfortable chairs from the living room had been moved so they could all three be comfortable in the evenings. B.C. was propped up, enjoying part of his day's allotment of sitting-up time. He looked awful, but it was mostly just the blue-white light of the television in the otherwise dark room.

"Say, I got to thinking," he said when a commercial came on. "Tuck, you'd ought to get yourself enrolled in the high school here, finish out your year anyway, and get the rest of those credits you was talking about. Looks like the three of us are going to be stuck here till at least June or July, and no use in you wasting this time completely."

"I'm supposed to be helping Grace," Tuck said, glancing over the bed at the woman beyond it, squinting over her afghan crocheting. "It doesn't seem like I'm really doing all that much helping, I guess. But I want to. Y'all are feeding me and housing me, and I want to help."

Grace said, "There's really not all that much to do, honey. It's just that somebody needs to be in hollering distance of B.C. till he can get around better, and with you here I don't need to feel like I'm tied to the bedpost. Don't worry, you're doing your share. If you don't, I'll take to beating on you."

Tuck grinned, but the grin faded as the original question came back into her head. "I don't know about school, though, B.C. Not that I'd mind going back for a while, since I can't rodeo this spring and it would be a good time to be working toward that diploma, like you say. But, two things. One, I feel like I've got to work on Indigo's training, put as much time as I possibly can in on her, if she's going to be a barrel horse by the time we're back on the circuit. And after that session with Betsy Bounce this afternoon I can see Indigo and me have a long old row to hoe before we earn a penny, can-chasing.

"And furthermore than that, wouldn't the school here have to have some sort of records from my old school? If they got in touch with my school in Springfield, I know the principal there would tell the state juvenile authorities, and they'd come after me quicker than scat and haul me back to Springfield."

The idea of leaving here and Indigo was so dreadful that her head couldn't hold it. She shivered.

"What are you going to do, then?" Grace asked reasonably. "You said you wanted to graduate high school, and you'll never have a better chance to finish off the work than right now, while we're grounded."

The commercials ended, and Tuck was spared an answer until the next commercial break, when she said, "Maybe what I'll do is call somebody tomorrow at the school, not tell them who I am, but just sort of ask a few questions. I still think there's a way of getting the diploma just by passing some kind of test, and maybe for that they don't need past records."

Tuck stayed in the house all morning playing euchre with B.C., while Grace made a start at spading up a place for a vegetable garden. Most years they didn't bother with a garden, she explained to Tuck, since they were on the road so much of the time. Tuck, listening behind the words, realized that money was tight for Grace and B.C. right now, and the garden food might make a big difference.

"If you don't mind me asking," she said as B.C. dealt another hand, "how much do rodeo clowns make? I mean, is that your only income?"

"Oh, I get around a hundred, hundred-fifty a day, depending on the rodeo."

Tuck's eyes widened. Five days at that rate and she could pay off Indigo and get her buckle back. "They ever let women be clowns?"

He shook his head. "I don't know if it's a rule or not,

but I never knew any. Too dangerous. And anyhow, it's not really that much of a living when you figure the number of days you're not working. And the travel expenses and all. Oh, we're not in too bad a shape, if that's what you were worrying about. We got this place and it's paid for, and I'll make maybe four, five thousand a year from my cows, enough to pay property taxes and a little left over, so the clown money carries us pretty decent most of the time. You going to play that hand or memorize it?"

╱ Late in the morning, while B.C. was napping, Tuck walked to the phone. Several times. She looked up the number of the consolidated high school three miles away, out on the highway. Eventually she dialed the number and asked for the principal's office, and asked her circumlocutory questions. The secretary started out helpfully, saying, yes, you could take a G.E.D. test if you qualified, and yes, there was a place in Ponca City where the tests were given, but then she got cagey when Tuck refused to give her name, and the whole thing ended in a stalemate. Tuck hung up determined to put off the education part of her life's goals until things got less complicated.

After lunch dishes, Tuck headed for Indigo with a square yard of old quilted mattress pad Grace had cut for her to use as a saddle pad. Indigo was grazing among the oil barrels. Tuck left the pad on the fence with the saddle and got a scoop of oats for bait. Indigo walked toward her as soon as the mare caught sight of the grain scoop. When the oats had all disappeared up the long black head, Tuck tied the mare to the fence and set about her with brush and rubber curry comb.

The winter coat was beginning to come loose. Tuck

101

brushed a cloud of it into the air and ended up with a mostly-still-woolly horse with a few areas on her neck where the close, shiny summer coat lay exposed. It was darker in color than the mostly-white winter woolens. Tuck got down nose to neck with the mare for a closer look, fascinated by the almost perfect alternation of black and white hairs that created the illusion of blue.

"Okay now, listen to me. Are you listening? We're going to put this saddle on, but it's not a bucking saddle. See? It's got a horn, that's how you can tell the difference. So it doesn't mean bucking, it just means riding like we've been doing, okay? This is the pad."

She lay the quilted square across Indigo's back. The mare paid no attention.

Sucking in a breath and letting out a prayer, Tuck eased the saddle off the fence and showed it to Indigo. The mare stiffened all over and rolled her eyes at it. For several long minutes Tuck stood in front of Indigo, awkwardly balancing the weight of the saddle in her arms and waiting for the horse to calm down. Indigo didn't calm down, nor get any worse, but the saddle got to weighing about six hundred pounds. Tuck set it down a minute while her arms recovered, then decided to go on to the next step and see what happened.

Only she'd never saddled a horse before. When she heaved the thing up toward Indigo's back, the offside stirrup and the cinch got in the way. She lowered it to the ground again, flopped stirrup and cinch over the saddle's seat like she'd seen Mason do, and tried again.

"Whoa now, take it easy."

Indigo shied away from it. Tuck followed till the

102

mare was up against the fence, and managed to drop the saddle onto the pad. Indigo's back hunched ominously and her ears flattened. Tuck murmured and neck-scratched and held the saddle horn with one hand as the dance began. Side to side, back to the end of the rope and up to the fence Indigo moved as though looking for the cowboy to drop on her and the chute gate to open.

Eventually the mare slowed down enough for Tuck to move around to her other side, lower the cinch and stirrup gently, then make a clumsy attempt at tightening the cinch at least enough to hold the saddle in place. She was pretty sure she didn't have the knot right in the cinch strap, but at least things were holding together. She untied the rope and led Indigo back and forth along the fence, trying to keep her going as quietly and smoothly as possible.

Indigo started out bucking. She couldn't do too much at walking speed with Tuck hauling her head up, but she gave it her best shot anyhow. When she wasn't trying to buck she was trying to twist her head around to see and sniff the saddle. She couldn't seem to figure out this combination of wearing a saddle and not being allowed to buck, which, to her, was what the saddle was supposed to mean.

After a while Tuck unsaddled, exchanged halter for hackamore, and got on board, mildly disappointed at being back to bareback but not really surprised. "If it was easy, anybody could do it," she muttered.

And there was her barrel course. Her own training course just like all the other racers had at home to train on. Well, maybe rustier and weedier than the rest of them, but a start, anyhow.

With pounding heart Tuck steered Indigo toward their first barrel, just walking, just teaching her the pattern. The mare cocked her head at the barrel and walked around it cautiously, not getting within six feet of the thing. Tuck didn't push. They circled it clockwise, then walked toward the next, the barrel on the left-hand side of the triangle. This one they circled counterclockwise, and Indigo walked a shade closer to it. She wanted to speed up after that, and Tuck was tempted, but she resisted for both of them and kept it to a walk. Third barrel, again counterclockwise, and this time no sign of fear from the mare. Out of that turn they came headed straight down the course, between the first two barrels toward what would have been the finish line if there'd been one. Now Tuck let her out into a trot.

"Hey, you are wonderful," she crowed, hugging Indigo's neck just as though the horse had done something smart.

Around they went again. This time they jogged through the pattern. The mare went wide at first but was tightening her turns by the third barrel. Tuck let her lope in the home stretch.

Again they ran the course, and again and again, still trotting, working on turning as tightly as possible around each barrel, then having a little run coming home. By about the sixth or seventh time, Tuck was sure she was feeling a quickening in the mare, a watching for the barrels, and the beginning of Indigo's own maneuvering independent of rein pressure against her neck. Tuck wanted to whoop her elation at the top of her lungs, wanted to keep on going around and around, but she figured it might be smarter to stop before Indigo started getting tired of doing it. Keep a little edge for next time. For the rest of the afternoon they just rode, around the pasture and down the lane and back, and then a little along the dirt road although Tuck was nervous about traffic appearing suddenly. She was also concerned about how much gravel travel Indigo's long, chipped, unshod feet could take.

A little after four Betsy and Buttons appeared. Tuck held her breath as she introduced Indigo, telling herself she didn't really care what the little squirt thought of her horse, and caring painfully.

"Hey, she's neat," Betsy said.

"Well, maybe not *neat*," Tuck laughed, looking at the mop of mane, the moth-eaten coat, and the shaggy fetlocks, "but she's my friend, and I like her."

"I know what you mean." Betsy dismounted for a closer look. "She's got a nice head, good and wide between the eyes, not too heavy in the neck, good straight legs, short back. That's important. Those long, strung-out horses never seem to be able to get themselves around the turns. Good muscling in her thighs. Look at there, Tuck, how she's got as much muscling on the insides of her hind legs as on the outside. That's important. She must be at least part quarter horse, I'd say. Maybe all. And she's going to be a beautiful color when she sheds out. You were really lucky to get her."

Tuck couldn't talk for grinning. Heck, the little squirt really did know horses!

Tuck told Betsy about the saddle problems, and they

agreed that slow and easy was best. Betsy smiled but didn't laugh out loud when she saw the saddle. At that point Tuck decided she had a friend. They tied the horses while Betsy paced off the distances between the barrels, and the distance from the last barrel to where the finish line should be, and they marked it with a couple of rocks. Tuck had a lesson in cinch-strap tying. She practiced on Buttons till she had it down pat, and her knots were as neat and flat as they needed to be. Then Betsy and Tuck took turns running the barrels, Betsy for speed and Tuck for pointers on things she might be doing wrong.

"Hard to tell, while you're still in the trotting stage," Betsy said, "but you both look fine to me. Indigo drops her head and shoulder going into the turns like she should, and she looks like she's fairly agile, all except on that first barrel. She takes that one wide every time, doesn't she?"

"Yeah, I noticed that. What causes that?"

Betsy shrugged. "Probably she's just not suppled enough in that direction yet. She's probably left-legged."

Tuck hooted, then realized Betsy wasn't joking. "Really?"

"Sure. Most horses are stiffer on one side than the other, at least when you first start working them. They'll always canter on their left lead if they have a chance, or whatever side they're best at. You just have to keep exercising them in both directions, doing tighter and tighter turns till they get loosened up."

Eventually Betsy got around to saying the magic words. "You want to try a run on Buttons?"

"Yes!"

106

They let the stirrups down so low they looked like training wheels, then Tuck handed over Indigo's reins and stepped up onto the pony. She laughed aloud at the shortness of him.

"Okay now, get a good hold on the saddle horn so he doesn't lose you around the turns, and don't jerk on his mouth whatever you do. Lean into the corners but not too far. Slow him down a couple of strides before you get to the barrel, or just let him do it himself, he knows how."

"Right, Captain." But Tuck felt less cocky as she turned the pony toward the starting line and began to feel the electricity in him. She got herself a death grip on the horn. "Okay, here we go," she muttered. "Let her rip."

As she spun Buttons around and headed him toward the first barrel, her head whiplashed back under the force of his leap. Her grip on the horn was all that kept her on board. Before she could get her breath they were at the barrel, starting a churning spin around it. Pain cracked through her as her right knee hit the barrel and sent it spinning. Buttons leaped on.

Now Tuck was hunched forward and driving him with flapping legs and elbows. They did a perfect turn around the second barrel, a too-wide one around the third, but the dash for home was the most exciting three seconds Tuck had ever experienced. When she got off her legs and hands were shaking, her face was flushed, and her heart belonged to the barrels.

For the rest of that week Indigo's lessons became the only real part of the day for Tuck. She was out before breakfast giving the mare saddle practice, just wearing it and walking in it and getting used to the idea. Then again after lunch—first saddle lessons, then riding, still bareback but getting closer all the time.

They began the workouts with several trot-throughs of the barrel course. Then they shifted to the other end of the pasture for cantering, trotting, cantering again in endless circles. Only occasionally did Indigo buck, and that was usually when she got started cantering on the wrong lead and got her legs tangled.

Leads were Tuck's big project for now, learning to tell from the rocking body beneath her whether Indigo was leading out with her right or left foreleg, learning how to make the horse take the lead Tuck wanted her to. It wasn't easy, especially since it still took quite a bit of Tuck's energy just to stay on. But every day she could feel her thigh muscles getting stronger, her grip more secure. She was learning to make her lower back relax and swing with Indigo's stride, even trotting, and it was a fantastic feeling.

But the leads were still a pain in the neck. Betsy had stressed the importance of being able to switch Indigo's leads instantaneously during a race, since no horse can turn a tight corner unless it's leading with the inside leg.

At first they cantered in fairly big figure-eight loops, slowing to a trot for a few steps at the crossover, then changing leads for the next circle. But once on the third day, and three times on the fourth, Indigo shifted from left to right lead at the cross point without breaking gait, and it was wonderful. Like waltzing, thought Tuck, who had never waltzed nor wanted to. Flying lead changes! Al-

108

ready! Proof in anybody's book that Indigo was a good horse. A perfect horse.

On Friday Tuck tried the acid test—changing leads on the straightaway, with no curved path to help cue Indigo. They started out cantering the length of the far fence, first on the left lead, then coming back again on the right. Trouble was, Tuck was never completely sure whether Indigo had actually taken the cues Tuck gave her for which lead to be on. It hadn't been hard to tell when they were going around in circles; a wrong lead and the horse would have stumbled. But now it was different. She tried looking down at Indigo's shoulders like Betsy suggested, but she couldn't tell which one was out front, and looking down made her lose her balance.

"Well, we'll try it anyway. What the heck."

She lined Indigo up along the fence, then reined to the right and tapped the horse's side with her right heel. Left lead? It felt like it. Maybe. . . . Halfway along the fence Tuck pulled in slightly on the reins, then bent the mare leftward with heel and hand. Yes! She could feel the shift, the little half-beat, then the canter continuing on a slightly altered angle of the horse's body.

Tuck's elation was so great at the end of the workout that she ached for someone to share it with. Betsy was staying late at school today for some committee meeting and wouldn't be over. In her overflow of excited energy Tuck rode up to the fence where the saddle was, dismounted, saddled up, and got on, not letting herself think whether this was the time. She just got on.

Indigo's back rose in an ominous hump beneath Tuck. Quickly Tuck reined the mare toward the barrels.

109

Indigo moved stiffly, but she moved, trotting on her fore-legs, cantering behind, confused as to whether she wasn't supposed to be bucking.

"Good girl, you're doing fine." Tuck stroked the mare's neck. She slowed Indigo to a walk through the barrel pattern. The mare cocked her head at the barrels as she passed them, seeming to remember now what this was all about.

When they walked out of the pattern there were clean streaks down Tuck's cheeks from her eyes to her mammoth grin.

While Tuck was in the barn serving dinner to the most perfect horse God ever turned off the assembly line, a car drove in, and a woman got out and was admitted to the house.

8

Tuck stopped cold in the living room, her hackamore slung around her neck, a joyful announcement frozen in her mouth. Grace and a strange woman sat stiffly in the living room, and that alone warned Tuck. Any friendly visitor would be in B.C.'s room. And besides, Tuck's radar told her this one was a social worker. She knew the look; the carefully concerned face, the carefully casual suit, the slim briefcase on the floor beside her feet.

Panic washed through Tuck. This is it. They're going to take me back! Indigo!

She took a half-step backward and her hand went to the hackamore, clutched it against her chest. Mentally she measured the distance to the barn, to Indigo, then where? Across country? No, it was all fenced.

The woman lifted her round, bland face toward Tuck and smiled. "You must be Ann Tucker, right?"

Tuck scowled. "No. Sorry. You got the wrong party."

In a voice that was gentle for her, Grace said, "Tuck, she already knows who you are. This is Mrs.—what'd you say your name was?"

"Mrs. Bevins. I'm from the State Juvenile Division, Ann. Come in. Sit down. We need to talk."

All the air went out of Tuck, and all the strength. She folded onto the arm of the davenport, by Grace. "How did you find me?" she asked in a hopeless monotone.

"We had a call from the secretary at the high school here, Ann. I believe you'd called and inquired about taking some classes there, and she got suspicious when you wouldn't tell her who you were. And then she'd heard one of the girls in the neighborhood here telling her friends about a Tucker girl staying with the Olmsteads. So I thought I'd better come by and check it out. They're pretty worried about you back in Springfield, you know."

"Hah."

From B.C.'s room came his voice. "Who's out there? We got company, Grace? Bring 'em in here. I'm awake now."

Grace glanced from Tuck to Mrs. Bevins. "Let's move in there. My husband's got to be in on this, and he's laid up."

They shifted to B.C.'s room, and Grace explained to him what was going on.

He hoisted himself as high up against the pillows as he could and took charge. "Now you listen here. Tuck is our friend and our good right hand, and we ain't about to let you haul her off to someplace she don't want to be. So you can just pack up your papers and peddle them someplace else."

Grace said, "No call to be rude to the lady, B.C. She's got her job to do. Now then," she turned to Mrs. Bevins, "it's plain and simple. Tuck wants to be here. She wasn't

112

happy in Springfield; she don't want to go back, and we don't want her to either. She's got her a horse here now, and a job working with us, and a home with people that want her. It'd be stupid to up and drag her back to that group home in that city, now wouldn't it?"

"But Ann is out of state, Mrs. Olmstead."

"No, she ain't. She may be out of one state, but she's into another one, so what difference does it make? Oklahoma any worse a state for a kid to be in than Missouri?"

"No. Of course not." Mrs. Bevin's professional cool began to crack. "But the point is, Ann is a ward of the state of Missouri. They are responsible for taking care of her, and—"

B.C. snorted. "Tuck don't need no state of Missouri to take care of her. She can do just fine on her own. Do you know that girl's taken a rodeo bronc and gentled it down into a saddle horse? She's been working, earning her way along, helping my wife and me. Why, shoot, she don't need the state of Missouri *or* Oklahoma or anything else."

Mrs. Bevin's voice was edged with exasperation. "That may very well be, Mr. Olmstead, but the fact remains that until she is eighteen or legally adopted Ann is the responsibility of the state of Missouri. Our Interstate Division, therefore, has the responsibility of returning her to her legal residence in Springfield."

Tuck's head went back and forth as though she were watching a tennis match. Only she herself was the ball. She couldn't breathe or think.

A look flashed between Grace and B.C. Together they said, "We'll adopt her."

Tuck's jaw dropped. For sixteen years of soaring

113

hopes and disappointments nobody had ever said those three magic words. And now here it was. Happening!

Mrs. Bevins scowled thoughtfully. "This isn't something to be decided on the spur of the moment, you know. It's a very big decision, a big responsibility. A teenage girl, well, there can be all sorts of problems, drugs, pregnancy—"

Tuck lunged to her feet. "Hey!"

B.C. rared up on his pillow. "Now you looka-here, you got no call to say things like that about a girl you don't even know. Tuck ain't that kind, and I think you owe her an apology."

The woman flushed. "I'm sorry if I offended anyone, but facts are facts, and drugs and pregnancies are serious and frequent problems among runaway teenagers that we deal with."

Finally Tuck found her voice. "I'm not a runaway, Mrs. Bevins. I'm a run-*to*." She explained as best she could about the rodeoing and how she'd come to hook up with Grace and B.C.

Mrs. Bevins frowned, but it looked to Tuck more like a thinking frown than a mad one. "Tell you what. I'll write up a report on all this and send it back to Springfield and see what they have to say about it. The fact that Ann is sixteen, old enough to work, and apparently has strong ideas about what she wants to do with her life"—she paused as though puzzling why anyone would want to rodeo—"may make a difference in their decision. We'll just have to wait and see. In the meantime, can I depend on you not to leave here?" She leveled an iron look at Tuck.

114

Tuck nodded.

"All right then. For now, this seems to be the best place to leave you, Ann, until we decide what's to be done. There will probably be a caseworker out to make a report on you"—she looked at Grace and B.C.—"on your suitability as a foster home for Ann."

When the woman was finally out of the house and gone, a long, charged look snapped among the three of them in the little bedroom. It was Tuck who spoke first.

"That'll teach you to pick up hitchhikers."

As the days of April leafed past her, Tuck flung herself into whatever she could find to do with an almost savage energy. She mowed lawn. She jerked weeds out of the new sprouting garden and flung them over her shoulder. She spent long hot afternoons with Grover, bouncing around the perimeters of huge pastures in the pickup, with piles of fence posts and rolls of barbed wire. She learned how to dig post holes and fill and tamp and wire-stretch, how to wham home the fence staples at an angle so the barbed wire couldn't slip through, and how to sweat and survive and relish the work.

It was as if a loose, convenient friendship had hardened that afternoon in B.C.'s bedroom. An offer had been made, an offer so overwhelming that Tuck's instinctive reaction had been to strike out against it, to protect herself from the unbearable likelihood that it wasn't for real. But it was. B.C. kept on repeating it even after the woman had gone, and Grace was right with him. They were willing to take her. Permanent. Willing to go through whatever trouble and expense might be involved in getting legal custody of Tuck, and for no other reason than that they liked her.

The implications were staggering.

Tuck Tucker was *likeable*. Maybe loveable, though that word didn't get tossed around easily.

B.C. and Grace had put themselves on the line for Tuck, and now she felt a surging necessity to earn their affection. It was as though by doing the work B.C. would have been doing if he could, Tuck was buying her way into the family.

B.C. was out of bed now, so Tuck was freed from the nursing part of the work. He sat most of the day in a lawn chair on the porch, reading his westerns or doing what little repair jobs he could do from there, or just napping or watching Tuck's labors. Sometimes he wrote ideas for new clown routines in a spiral notebook or sketched new patterns for clown faces.

Once in a while when his eyes followed her, Tuck sensed that he was remembering past times when, maybe, their son had been her age and doing the same jobs around the place. But B.C. never talked about Brent, and he didn't encourage Grace to either, so Tuck figured there was some trouble there that she didn't know about and wasn't supposed to.

She didn't dwell on it. Her life was splitting at the seams. She was up and out early every morning, working Indigo. She threw herself into whatever the day's job was, and in the late afternoons she worked Indigo again with Betsy and Buttons, either at home or at Betsy's. Her energy seemed limitless, but only part of it came from being happy and fitting into the life she was living. The rest of it came from fear that any day Mrs. Bevins could show up again and rip it all away from her.

As hot weather settled in seriously, Indigo shed out the last of her winter coat and turned beautiful. Her slate blue body had shiny highlights on its curves now, and the black head looked like an oil painting. On the day that the farrier was scheduled to come to Betsy's house to shoe Buttons for the coming show season, Tuck rode Indigo over and had her hooves trimmed. She couldn't quite bring herself to cut into her money thirty dollars' worth for shoes, but a six-dollar trim job made Indigo's feet look like a serious using horse's rather than a bronc's. And the farrier assured Tuck that the mare had good, tough feet that didn't need shoes anyway so long as she wasn't ridden on gravel too much.

After the man had packed his pickup and driven off, Tuck and Betsy got out the electric horse clippers and ganged up on Indigo. They shaved the tufts off her pasterns and the shags off the backs of her legs. They ran the clippers along the mare's jowls and got rid of the straggles and whiskers. Then, somewhat reluctantly on Tuck's part, they started on Indigo's mane.

"She'll look a lot neater," Betsy insisted as the locks began to fall, "and she'll rein better for you without all that hair in the way."

It was a slow job. The mane was bushy, and Indigo didn't much like the feel of the clippers on her crest, but eventually the ground was covered with black horsehair, and Indigo stood in all her glory, a barrel horse. Tuck stood back and sucked in her breath at the difference it made. Indigo's shaggy bronc look was entirely gone now. A neat pencil-line of black outlined the attractive arch of her neck. Tuck thought suddenly of Coppertone.

"Shall we give 'em a work?" Betsy's voice cut into Tuck's reverie.

They saddled up and went their separate ways, loping in easy circles until the horses were sufficiently warm and limber. Then Tuck held the stopwatch while Betsy did a run. Twenty-three seconds. Buttons' first runs were always slow. She handed the watch to Betsy, but not for timing purposes since she hadn't yet begun to run Indigo seriously.

"Go," Betsy yelled. Tuck booted Indigo into an easy gallop, concentrating on the precise spot to aim at approaching the first barrel and on Indigo's shortening stride coming into the turn. They rounded the barrel beautifully, the mare's shoulder never more than a foot away from the metal rim. When they were halfway to the second barrel Tuck cued for the change of lead and felt, with a distinct thrill, the lightning shift in the mare's carriage. The change had been made at the instant when it would cause the least delay.

Indigo was off to the next barrel, still galloping comfortably, watching where she was going, feeling what Tuck was doing up there on her back. They came around slightly wider than the first time but still neatly. This time there was no need for a lead change as they came away from the turn, only for acceleration toward the final barrel. Tuck concentrated intently on the approaching barrel, seeking the exact instant to apply the brakes.

She waited a fraction too long, overshot by a stride, but spun the mare and let her out for a fast run home.

As they trotted back toward Betsy, the younger girl was shaking her head. "I still think you're making a mistake letting her gallop through it slow like that. You're going to have trouble getting her to race."

Tuck's face set in stubbornness. "And *I* still think it's better for her to know exactly what she's supposed to do, and how to do it, before I push for speed. I think control is more important than flat-out speed. But," she said as she pulled in her breath, "I also think she's ready for a real run now."

Betsy took another turn, shaving a second off her first run time. Then Tuck handed her the watch and said, "Okay now, we're going to try a real run, so time us."

She took Betsy's bat and held it awkwardly in her right hand. "Okay, this is serious now," she muttered to Indigo. She turned the mare in a quick circle behind the starting posts, riding vigorously, trying to excite Indigo and get her dancing like Buttons did before a run.

"Go," she yelled, and spun Indigo onto the course. Whooping and flailing with the bat, she drove toward the first barrel.

But Indigo, startled back into bronc memories by the clamor, began to buck. Tuck stayed on for two and a half jumps.

"Seven seconds," Betsy called cheerfully.

"Oh, shut up."

Tuck dusted herself off and tried again, this time without the yelling and the bat, just driving for speed with her legs. Indigo came through the starting line galloping nervously, her ears twitching in her uncertainty. But before she'd reached the first barrel she settled in. The turn

119

wasn't as neat as their slower ones had been in the past, but it was good and quick, and the shift to left lead came precisely when it was supposed to. Tuck's heart sang.

Now, suddenly, Indigo caught onto the game. She flat-out ran to the next barrel, settling herself into the turn with no help from Tuck at all, then ripped up the triangle to the last barrel and around it and flew home!

The flap-covered saddle horn punched Tuck's stomach all through the neck hug Indigo got. The shaved mane felt spikey against Tuck's face. She sat up singing, not even caring what the time had been. Indigo was a barrel horse! It wasn't a dream anymore.

Betsy rode over, waving the stop watch. "Hey! That was an eighteen. See? I told you you should roach her mane."

May came, and the Olmstead table bloomed with garden lettuce, fresh peas, early beans. The fencing was finished, and all the calves were born, and the first cutting of hay was turned into giant jelly rolls of pale gold as tall as Tuck's head, scattered across the hay fields. Tuck and Indigo went for long loping rides across the stubbly fields, doing figure eights around the giant bales. Sometimes they rode through the pastures playing cowboy, but there really wasn't much to do. The calves weren't in any danger from anything, and their mothers didn't appreciate visitors.

B.C. spent his afternoons inside now, having gotten hooked on first one soap opera, then another. "Crazy fools," he'd mutter. "What man in his right mind's going to be wasting that much time away from his business just to get messed up in all that gossip and dog-fighting among those women?" But still he watched.

As the days lengthened and grew hotter, Indigo's workouts were done earlier in the morning and later in the evening. Tuck and Betsy began riding after supper rather than before. The middle part of the day, when it was too hot even for weed pulling in the garden, became the good time, the lazy time. Tuck read B.C.'s neglected western novels or listened through the open window to the television stories going on in the living room. The folding chaise lounge on the porch became hers for the afternoon hours.

One day in the third week of May a state caseworker came to do what she called a profile of the Olmsteads. She looked around the house and asked specific questions about income and insurance and other children in the family and how long B.C. would be out of work. She seemed to keep gnawing at the dangerous nature of B.C.'s profession and the marginal family finances, but eventually she closed her clipboard and said, "I believe I can give you a favorable report."

Grace and B.C. and Tuck looked at one another, then at her. "What does that mean?" Grace asked.

"Just that in my opinion this is an adequate foster home situation for Ann. A little more financial stability would have been better, but there seems to be a good relationship going here, and Ann appears to be happy and adjusting well to her current situation, and that's the main thing."

"What does that mean?" Grace demanded again. "Does that mean we can adopt her?"

The woman frowned slightly. "This is just a preliminary home check, you understand, just to ascertain

121

whether Ann should be returned to Springfield or allowed to stay where she is. Adoption would be another matter. In view of Ann's age, the fact that she's almost old enough to be independent, a foster home situation might make more sense than going through the expensive legalities of an adoption, name change, all that. If the state agreed, you would become Ann's foster parents and legal guardians, and the state would pay you a small monthly allotment for her care, until she was eighteen."

"And she could stay with us as long as she wants?" Grace demanded.

The woman nodded.

B.C. said, "We offered to adopt you, Tuck, and the offer holds. It's up to you."

"Now don't you go dumping a thing like that on her young shoulders," Grace scolded. "We'll all talk it over and decide."

But Tuck shook her head. By now she knew how little money there was between their bank balance and nothing. It wasn't a whole lot more than she had herself, and that would have fit in a pig's eye and left room for lashes. If adoption meant paying out and foster care meant a check coming in, then there was no deciding to it.

"We'll take foster," she announced. Her eyes met Grace's, then B.C.'s. She hoped they understood how much she'd have rather had the adoption.

As the woman stood to leave she said, "Well now, Ann, I can't make any promises at this early stage, but I'd say your chances are pretty good that you'll be allowed to stay here." As Tuck's grin began to spread the woman added, "And just between you and me, I think you did a fine job of picking out parents. I expect you're going to turn out to be one of those persons who takes life by the tail and swings it her way. I'll be back in touch as soon as I have some definite news for you."

That night Indigo got a vacation. Grace and B.C. and Tuck scrubbed themselves up and drove in to Ponca City for steaks at the Bonanza Steak House, then to a western bar where Grace danced with everybody in sight, and Tuck drank cokes and stomped and clapped and did a little dancing of her own, and B.C. told jokes that weren't even funny but had the place rolling anyway just from the sheer joy he radiated.

It was the best night of Tuck's life. Bar none.

9

"Hooeee, I don't think I've got the nerves for this sport," Tuck said, wiping her face on her shirt sleeve. She stood beside the pickup, talking in through the window to B.C. and Grace. The truck was parked beside the arena in a county fairground twenty miles from home. It was just a small local show, Tuck told herself again, nothing to get all up in a heaval about, just because it was Indigo's first run in public and their whole futures hung on how she did today.

The mare grazed near Tuck's foot, her reins over Tuck's arm. A little ways away, Betsy and Buttons were warming up and receiving last minute instructions from Betsy's parents, who didn't know what they were talking about but liked to give instructions anyway. Tuck reckoned Indigo was warmed up enough.

Today she wore an old straw western hat of Grace's for sun protection, and her better jeans and shirt, and boots that had left home polished, anyway.

Grace leaned forward against the steering wheel to see around B.C. to Tuck. "What did you enter?"

"Junior Barrels, that'll be up next after the flag races, and Open Barrels."

Grace nodded and settled back to watch. Within the arena the three barrels were in place, but being put to a slightly different use. The two side barrels each held a bucket of sand on top. One at a time the flag racers came charging into the arena, galloped past the first sand bucket, and snatched out of it a small flag, which they then carried at full tilt around the end barrel to the other side barrel, where they stabbed the flag down into that sand bucket. Or tried to. Tuck would have enjoyed watching the flag race if she hadn't been so sick with nervous excitement about her own race.

In the ring behind her, the halter and pleasure classes were going on. Tuck hardly noticed them, nor the other horses being ridden or led among the parked vehicles scattered across the dusty plain. She could think of nothing beyond Indigo and the coming race.

Finally the flag races ceased, and their winners were announced. Tuck mounted and rode Indigo toward the arena entrance with Betsy and Buttons and a swarm of gathering Junior Barrelers. They were almost all girls, Tuck noticed, some of them quite young looking. She was glad to see that several rode ponies. They wouldn't be the competition, she sensed. It would be the other, older girls on the tough-looking quarter horses. Those would be the challenge. They were looking her over. She was a new face; Indigo was a complete unknown. Tuck could feel her measure being taken by a dozen eyes. Casually she dropped her hand down over the flapping saddle horn cover and sat up straighter.

125

A man on foot walked among them. "Okay now, here's your order. Seventy-two, seventy-six, seventy-seven, seventy-nine, eighty-three—" he read on. Tuck relaxed slightly. She was seventy-seven, third up, right after Betsy. Perfect. Not the first in, but not a long wait either.

She turned Indigo and booted her into a gallop away from the arena, spun her around, and galloped back, to be sure the mare was limbered up and eager to run. She was.

The announcer said. "First up in the Junior Barrel race, riders eighteen and under, is number seventy-two. Seventy-six on deck."

Tuck rode over to where she could watch. Seventy-two got off to a bad start, going wide at the first barrel and knocking over the second. Tuck cheered silently.

"Seventy-six up, seventy-seven on deck. No time, for seventy-two," the announcer called.

Tuck missed seeing Betsy's run because she was getting herself into the on-deck position, ready to charge in. She thought fleetingly about throwing up, but there wasn't time.

Buttons shot past and churned to a stop.

"Time on number seventy-six, twenty and oh two three. Seventy-seven up, seventy-nine on deck."

Tuck went rigid. It was time. Now.

She felt Indigo begin to dance beneath her. It was like revving up a race car's engine before slamming it into gear. The mare's neck lathered in excitement.

She wants to go, Tuck realized. In that flash she, too, wanted to go. Her fear broke away and the glory poured out.

She spun Indigo toward the starting gate and with a

126

huge leap they were off. The first barrel came at them too fast. Tuck braked. Indigo sat on her tail and churned dirt and got herself around it better than Tuck had hoped for, leaping away from the spin on her left lead and flattening out for the run. At the second barrel their turn was perfect. Tuck felt the beauty of it as Indigo dropped speed at precisely the right instant and laid into the turn. The barrel brushed Tuck's leg but didn't rock.

They leaped away, skidded a bit at the last barrel, then shot for home, Indigo flattened out and flying, Tuck flapping her wings. Well beyond the electric eye at the gate, she pulled up and turned to hear the voice of fate.

"Time on seventy-seven, seventeen and nine two three. That's the time to beat, so far."

Tuck glowed through Betsy's congratulations and through all the rest of the runs. She listened to the others' times and hoped hers would hold, but the main thing was that Indigo had done a good job. A *good* job. Good enough to tackle the Pro Rodeo circuit as soon as B.C. was healed. Maybe not good enough yet to knock off the Jonas of the world, but good enough to play in their ball park.

When they drove home that evening, Indigo sharing Buttons' trailer, Tuck was the proud possessor of two big rosettes, first place in Junior Barrels and third place in Open, where the competition had been seasoned adults on seasoned horses. Her jackpot winnings totaled sixty-three dollars and fifty cents.

It was a start.

Tuck lay on the chaise lounge on the front porch, her empty ice cream dish riding on her bare stomach. She

127

stared at the porch roof and let the sounds of the argument drift over her. There was a wasp nest being built up there in the corner. Have to get rid of it, she thought, yawning.

"Why would Jason murder his own child?" Grace yelled. "That doesn't make sense, you old fool."

B.C. yelled back, "He didn't *know* Emily was his, that's why. And she wasn't supposed to have died, only got kidnapped was all he intended. That makes more sense than your theory anyway. Natalie ain't got the morals of a goat, but she's a good person down under it all. She wouldn't hurt a child, especially not Jason's."

"Except she don't know Emily is Jason's either."

They both ended up laughing, and Tuck relaxed a shade. Tempers were beginning to get just a little short, with the hot weather and not enough to do. But that was about to end, thank goodness. Another week and they'd be on their way to Montana. The doctor had finally given grudging approval for B.C. to go back to work, and the Billings Rodeo was the first job B.C. had been able to line up.

Into the silence that followed the soap opera feud Tuck said, "What if we can't find anybody to haul Indigo?" It was her biggest fear. Grace had already made three long distance calls, trying to track down Mason or anyone else who might be heading toward Billings from this direction with a horse trailer. Hadn't made contact with anyone yet.

Grace said, "Don't you worry. We'll find someone."

"But what if we can't?"

"Then she'll have to stay home," Grace said flatly.

"Even if we could borrow a trailer we'd have no way to haul it behind the truck and our living trailer."

Tuck sighed and nodded and subsided. She knew it was the only alternative, and she knew she hated the idea. She'd have to stay behind then, too. She couldn't leave Indigo. She could stay here and continue to go to local shows with Betsy's family and continue to rake in jackpot money that barely covered expenses.

She and Betsy had been to four more shows since that first one, and even though Indigo was regularly in the money, the jackpots were just too small. There was her share of the gas money for the trip, and the thirty dollars for the shoes that Indigo finally needed badly. There was twenty-two dollars for a new saddle pad when the old quilt wore through and threatened saddle sores on Indigo's withers. There was eighteen dollars for new jeans when Tuck's old ones finally gave up and disintegrated where they rubbed the saddle. There was grain for Indigo since you can't run a racing machine on grass for fuel, and there were four kinds of shots and a Coggins test that Indigo had to have before she could travel.

What with all that, and entry fees of five to ten dollars for every race, Tuck's grand total was still lollygagging around the two-fifty mark, not much grander than before the five local shows. And it wasn't going to get much grander, she knew, not at these little shows, not till she and Indigo could dig into some Pro Rodeo races where a couple of good day-money wins would pay off the whole five hundred and get her buckle back.

And if she couldn't find transportation. . . .

129

The phone rang. Tuck held her breath and strained to listen to what Grace was saying, hoping hard that it was a ride for Indigo to Billings. Grace whooped as she hung up the phone and slammed out through the screen door, and Tuck sat up, ready for good news.

Grace bellowed, "Hey, B.C., we just had a baby. A six-foot-tall baby girl. That was the caseworker. Our foster parent application went through; all's we have to do is go in on Wednesday and sign the papers, and that long ole ugly kid over there is ours."

The three of them danced and stomped till the porch boards threatened to cave in under their boots and a lawn chair got knocked off into the bushes.

Tuck collapsed, panting, and looked from one to the other. "Life sure is funny."

"You found that out already, huh?" Grace shot back.

"Yeah. I run away from Springfield to get out of a foster home and into rodeoing, and here I am six months later, whooping and hollering at getting a new set of foster parents. You're my fifth set—"

B.C. said, "You kept trying till you got it right."

"Shut up, I'm being serious now. You're my fifth set, but this time we more or less picked each other out, didn't we? You're the only ones that feel like family to me. The others were just doing it for the money."

Seeing an uncomfortable look flash between Grace and B.C., Tuck hurried on. "I know you're doing it to help me, and not for the monthly checks. But still and all, I'm glad you'll be getting the money. It makes me feel like I'm helping out, some way."

B.C. had fished his chair out of the shrubbery by now

and sat back down in it. "You know, I been thinking about those checks. Seems to me that what we'd ought to do with them, *if* Tuck is willing since it's supposed to be for her food and clothes and what not, is to trade that old truck and trailer off for a down payment on a motor home of some kind. If we're all going to be going down the road together, permanent, from now on, we can't have our baby child sleeping in that truck and depending on other folks to haul her horse for her. What do you say, Mother?"

Grace grinned and smacked at his knee. "I say you're not as big a fool as you look like. That truck's about ready for a Christian burial anyhow, and a motor home'd give us a lot more room than our little trailer. *And* it could pull a horse trailer."

"If we had one," Tuck said, frowning. "You're not going to have enough money for a horse trailer, too. And besides, I should pay for the horse trailer. It's my horse. I've got about two-fifty saved up. Think that would make a down payment on a horse trailer?"

"An old beat-up one maybe," B.C. said. "But Tuck, now, are you sure you want your food and clothes money spent on a motor home? It'll mean no new duds for a good long while, probably not till you can earn 'em yourself, no money for schooling nor medical expenses nor anything like that."

Tuck stood up. She was too full of electricity to sit. "I plan to stay healthy, I'll get my schooling whatever way I can, and I wouldn't know a new dud if it bit me. Come on, let's go clean out the trailer!"

They started out the next morning, the three of them feeling almost formal riding in the cleaned-out junk-free

131

pickup, pulling an equally depersonalized trailer in its wake.

"The hard part will be the horse trailer," B.C. said as they coasted along toward Ponca City. "There are plenty of R.V. dealers around with lots full of motor homes, but a used horse trailer can be tough to find. New ones are so expensive people just don't like to let go of a used one if it's any good at all. Why, the new ones anymore will run you three thousand, thirty-five—"

"Hey," Tuck waved at him across Grace. "Stop. I just saw one. Pull over."

They pulled off onto the shoulder of the narrow highway, and Tuck jumped out. There, parked in the front yard of a farmhouse, stood a rust-colored two-horse trailer with a "For Sale" sign taped to it. Not rust colored, she realized, rust-covered. It looked awful. A hunk of broken trim stuck out from the side, and the license plate was held on by a twist of baling wire.

"Looks bad enough to be in our price range," B.C. muttered as a woman approached them from the house. Tuck was oblivious to the introductions. She looked at tires; they had some tread on them. She borrowed B.C.'s pocket knife and stabbed the wood planks of the floor. Knife blade went partway into the wood, but not all the way. She followed the wiring as far as she could with her eyes and her fingertips and found no frayed places. That exhausted her knowledge of trailers, what little knowledge she'd picked up from listening to cowboys talk about trailer problems they'd gotten into from not checking.

While B.C. was looking the trailer over, Tuck said to the woman, "How much you asking?"

132

"Four hundred."

She waited till B.C. had made his round and given her a small nod. "I'll give you two-fifty, cash."

Eventually they agreed on two-fifty down and another hundred within thirty days. "We'll be back to pick it up later," Tuck said as she shook the woman's hand.

Driving off again, Tuck's feelings came in layers of excitement and gloom. Her own horse trailer. But on the other hand, no money left at all, a hundred dollars into debt, and just two weeks left on the six months' limit for buying back the buckle.

Grace's hand closed on Tuck's knee. "Don't you worry, honey, once we get on the road again you ought to be able to earn some day money, anyhow, and two or three of those checks will pay off what you owe."

"If," Tuck muttered into the palm that held up her chin. "If Indigo's good enough. Just because she's in the money pretty regular at those little local shows, that doesn't mean she's going to be able to earn her way on the Pro circuit."

B.C. chirped, "Well, at least we got the wheels to get her there now. And I wouldn't sell that little mare short if I was you. She's got the speed she needs, and furthermore than that, she's got the control. You two have come a whale of a long way in the few months you been working her. A season or two on the Pro circuit and I'd bet you'll be doing as well as any of them."

"But I don't *have* a season or two, B.C. I have exactly two weeks."

It was late afternoon when they found what they were looking for, at the back of a lot full of recreational vehicles of all kinds and ages. It was a huge old Champion motor home covered with hunting and fishing decals and carrying an air of lumbering comfort about it. Across the front was a deep-dish driver's seat, walking space, then a two-seat wide bench. Before it spread a leatherette dashboard big enough to hold a party on and fitted with tape deck, beverage holders, and all sorts of pockets and gadgets. Above was a shelflike double-sized bed.

Back of that was the only door, the kitchen and bathroom area, and a surprising amount of storage cubby holes. Behind that was a roomy table with padded benches, and picture windows all around the back end. The salesman showed them how the booth part made into a broad double bed, with curtains across for privacy. B.C. checked the motor, the propane tanks, the water storage tanks, and the trailer hitch, and found nothing seriously wrong. He even discovered an awning that rolled out from the side to make a shady sitting area, and storage places underneath for lawn furniture and his fold-down chicken and cart rig.

With minimal dickering, truck and trailer were traded for the Champion, and they were on the road for home.

"How's it feel?" Tuck asked B.C. as he steered the thing onto the highway.

"Little like driving the county courthouse down the road, but I reckon I'll get used to it."

For the next three days, up until Wednesday when they would leave for Billings, Tuck threw herself into the job of de-rusting the trailer while Grace and B.C. puttered with the Champion, making up beds, stashing away dishes and books and clothes, and fixing the leak in the refrigera-

134

tor's drainage system. Tuck left her work only long enough for Indigo's workouts, morning and evening.

She dressed in some horrible old shorts of Grace's and immersed herself, almost literally, in rust remover. It was miserable hot work, even though the trailer was parked in the shade beside the house. Even Tuck's enthusiastic energy wasn't a match for the tenacity of that trailer's rust. But by evening of the second day B.C. pronounced the metal in good enough shape to hold paint. Tuck turned the garden hose on the hulk, which was now metal-colored with just traces of red. She hosed it inside and out, then collapsed on the grass, too pooped to worry about chiggers.

Next morning she was at it again, with a spray can of pale tan automobile paint that was almost the color of the motor home. This part of the job was so easy she sang all the way through it. The paint dried quickly, and by evening she was able to pack up. In the half of the trailer that Indigo wouldn't be using Tuck jammed four hay bales. She laid a thick bed of straw where Indigo would stand, and filled the feed rack with hay for the mare to munch while they traveled. Up front in the storage compartment went saddle, new pad, hackamore, long rope, buckets, brushes, and a bag of grain.

"There now," Tuck said with satisfaction as she dusted her hands on her seat, "all packed and ready to hit the road." Then she went inside and stuffed her wardrobe into her own little bag. That took two minutes, tops.

Next morning, as soon as the food was packed and Indigo loaded into the trailer, they were off. They detoured through Ponca City to sign the foster papers, then headed north toward Billings.

135

10

Tuck sat on Indigo just outside the arena entrance, waiting her turn for a run at the cans. It was Friday morning. The Champion had rolled into the rodeo grounds late yesterday afternoon, after two days of following the Rockies north into cool, clear summer air and rain-washed green countryside. Last evening Tuck had ridden Indigo around the grounds, in and out of the arena, to get the travel-stiffness out of the mare's legs and to reacquaint her with rodeo surroundings. The mare had spooked going in and out of the arena, as though expecting a bronc rider to land on her. This morning Tuck thought she seemed a hair more relaxed.

Several other barrel racers were in line ahead of Tuck for the practice runs. Tuck felt them watching her. They all knew each other. She was, at best, a vaguely familiar face that they couldn't quite place, on an unfamiliar horse. This Indigo with her sleek silvery hide and neat black line of roached mane looked nothing like the shaggy, platter-footed Blue Blazes who used to come out of the bucking chutes last winter.

Tuck felt different this time around, herself. Even if

136

those girls looking at her from on top of their streamlined, pastel-upholstered barrel racing saddles didn't know Tuck Tucker was a belonger, Tuck knew it. Whether or not Indigo was going to turn out to be good enough to play in this league, that remained to be seen. But the solid facts were that ole Tuck was no tumbleweed, this trip. She was rooted down to Grace and B.C. and that old Champion with the repainted horse trailer behind it. She had as much right here as any of them. She sat up straighter and prepared to look her competition in the eye, first chance she had.

"Hi." A girl's voice with a friendly lilt, behind Tuck.

It was Jona Riley, sitting her polished brown quarter horse with athletic ease, her twin pony tails hanging over her ears to make her look like a bespectacled spaniel. But she was smiling, which was more than the rest of them had given Tuck.

Tuck warmed to her and grinned. "Hi."

Jona looked at Indigo, then looked again. "That's that bronc you got last spring down in Oklahoma, isn't it? Boy, does she look different. You going to race her?"

Tuck nodded.

"She any good?"

Tuck shrugged. "We been winning pretty regular in the bush leagues, but I don't know about here."

"Your turn," Jona said, nodding toward the arena.

Tuck moved Indigo forward, then spun her around in a tight circle to get her awake and ready. Muscles bunched beneath the saddle, and tension came down the reins and into Tuck's body. Suddenly Tuck spun the mare and clapped her heels hard into Indigo's sides.

137

The mare leaped, then hesitated as she saw the bucking chutes on either side of her. She dipped her head and bucked once, then caught sight of the barrels and remembered. She flattened out and made her run, blind now to everything but those three barrels. Her homestretch run was enough to whip Tuck's face red with wind-chap and excitement.

After the run she went to the end of the line for a second shot at it. Jona joined her a few minutes later, after her own run. Tuck found herself liking Jona better than she had before. Probably because I'm getting more up to her level, Tuck decided.

"What's your horse's name?" Tuck asked.

"Scat. Well, his registered name is Poco Petronius, but Scat works better for a name to yell at him when we're running." Jona reached out a slim, fine-boned hand and stroked Scat's neck just once, but Tuck saw in that stroke the same kind of love she felt for Indigo.

"Looked like you had a little bucking problem for just a second there," Jona said.

"Yes. It was those chutes, I think. Where we've been racing they haven't had bucking chutes. She won't do it again."

And she didn't. Next time around, Indigo zeroed in on her number-one barrel and ran straight as raw spaghetti. No one was timing the practice runs, but it was a fine run, one of Indigo's best ever. Tuck could feel the rightness of it.

After their second run Tuck left the arena so as not to overdo it and make Indigo bored with the routine. She

138

rode around the stock pen area intending to talk to Merrill. There was still a little over a week left till the six months deadline for buying her buckle back, and she wanted to see if he'd brought it with him this trip, on the off chance that Indigo got lucky and won five hundred dollars' worth of day money in the six days of the Billings rodeo.

But the stock trucks that were spilling calves and bulls and broncs out into the pens were not Merrill trucks. Tuck turned Indigo and cantered around the parking area to where home was parked. Grace and B.C. had unfurled the awning on the Champion's side and were holding court beneath it. The porchlike rectangle of shade was cluttered with cowboys come to welcome B.C. back and to tell him and Grace what all they'd won and lost since March.

Mason was among them. He came out into the sun, squinted up at Tuck, and ran his hand over Indigo's shoulder.

"Hey there," he said.

Tuck nodded and grinned like a fool.

"B.C. tells me you've been racing your mare at the locals. Doing good with her, he says. Congratulations. She sure looks good."

"Thanks." It came over Tuck, seeing Mason again, that this was one of the main things she'd been hungry for all summer, that homely, sweet face squinting at her. But she couldn't enjoy it now, for worrying about Merrill.

She said, "I was just over looking for Merrill to ask him about my trophy buckle, you remember, that I traded for Indigo? But it was some other stock company."

Mason nodded. "Blain. Merrill doesn't have these northern rodeos usually. He's down around Texas this month. Did you get your five hundred dollars? Wasn't that how much you needed?"

Tuck shook and nodded her head all at once. "That was how much, but I don't have it. I'd win a little bit, and then it'd go for horseshoes or feed or whatever."

"Are you anywhere close?"

Tuck got down off of Indigo and began loosening her cinch. "Not what you could call real close, no. Two hundred and twenty in the hole. I owe a hundred more on the horse trailer, and then I had to borrow a hundred and twenty from B.C. for entry money for the six go-rounds here. And the deadline for getting the buckle back is next week, so it's now or never. Mason?"

"Yeah?"

She hauled off the saddle and upended it on the ground with the pad sunning on top. "You know Merrill pretty well, don't you? Would you say he's a generous sort of man?"

"I'd say he's tight as the vest on a statue, is what I'd say. I wouldn't count on any extensions of time from him, if that was what you were thinking."

She blew out a long gust of air and hope. "Well, I don't reckon I'll be getting my buckle back, then. So anyway. Catch me up on what you and Coppertone have been doing since spring. You going to get qualified for the National in time?"

While he talked, Tuck buckled on Indigo's halter and the two of them led the horse off in search of grass and

140

shade. In spite of the dark spot in her mood about the buckle, Tuck felt good. Good to be back.

Barrel racing was scheduled during the evening performance, the second event after the supper break, and following steer wrestling. Tuck kept Indigo moving, walking, jogging, in the shadows behind the stock pens where she could keep an eye on the progress of the steer wrestling and time her approach to the entrance accordingly. She was second on the lineup, just where she liked to be.

The last steer was thrown, and the judge's flag dropped.

"Time for the cowboy, twelve seconds two three two."

B.C. and another clown came into the arena to cut up and fill the time while the arena crew rolled the barrels into place.

"Here we go, old darling," Tuck muttered. "This is for the big money, now, and we're not going to have a split fraction of a second for bucking or any other kind of goofing up, you hear me? No losing your rear end on that right turn like you do sometimes. It's going to take three perfect turns and all the speed you've got if we're going to be in the money tonight. You got that?"

The announcer blared, "Our first barrel racer this evening, folks, is Miss Jona Riley from Liberal, Kansas. Ann Tucker on deck. And she's off!"

Jona and Scat shot into the arena. Tuck, from her spot on deck, just outside the entrance, squinted her eyes to watch the run. It looked good to her, but not perfect. Scat switched leads coming out of the turn, and it slowed him for just an instant. They came barreling down the home stretch run, through the electric eye timer, and out into the runway to slide to a stop beside Tuck and Indigo.

Jona's eyes met Tuck's and she shook her head. "We blew that one." Together they listened for the time.

"Time for Jona Riley, eighteen and oh three three."

Tuck swallowed. That would have been excellent time anyplace she'd raced that summer.

The gate man was motioning to her. She reined Indigo through her readying spin, hauled in a long breath, and charged.

No buck this time! Indigo flattened into the run. Tuck felt the mare concentrating on that first barrel. Leaning low over Indigo's neck, Tuck concentrated, too, on the approaching barrel and the strides beneath her. She breathed, "Go, go, go, go . . . now!" and leaned back into the stop at the end of the stride that brought the barrel to Indigo's nose.

She leaned into the turn with her horse, but remembered to give Indigo support behind with pressure from her outside leg, to help keep the horse's body from swinging wide. Indigo's shoulder came within six inches of the barrel rim and stayed there all the way around. Tuck sang inside.

As Indigo's head cleared the line of the barrel Tuck shifted her outside leg and rein hand, and Indigo leaped away on her left lead toward the second barrel. Again horse and rider concentrated on the approach, on just the instant to slam on the brakes to bring Indigo tight around the barrel. Tuck's toe touched metal, but the barrel remained upright. Off again. Speed now. Tuck urged Indigo into the run with all her soul. Brake again, hold the hindquarter spin with the outside leg, straight now, and away!

Tuck lay into the run. She yelled and war-whooped and flailed with legs and hands, and Indigo responded. Ears flattened, head down, the mare ran like she'd never run before.

When they'd slid to a stop outside the arena and Tuck's head cleared enough to hear with, what she heard was applause. Then everything grew still, waiting.

"Time for Ann Tucker, seventeen and oh oh five. That's the time to beat so far, folks."

It was the most beautiful sound Tuck had ever heard.

She rode to a spot along the rail where she could watch and listen to the remaining eight racers. Seventeen and oh oh five seconds. Good time. Very good time. Good enough to be in the money? She held her breath.

"Time for Gretchen Crowley, seventeen and three one six."

Tuck breathed.

"Time for Kim Elting, eighteen seconds even."

Tuck smiled a tight smile.

"Time for Jackie Anderson, seventeen and oh oh one."

There goes first place, Tuck thought. She grew tense.

"Time for Sue Schwartz, seventeen and oh four oh."

"Karen Doyle, seventeen seconds even."

There goes second place.

The next racer knocked over a barrel. No time. Only two left. Tuck clutched up so hard Indigo began to back in protest.

"Time for Cheryl Sebert, seventeen and . . . oh four nine."

I'm in the money, Tuck caroled to herself.

143

Last racer. A good run. Time, seventeen seconds and four sixty-seven thousandths.

Third place! One hundred twelve dollars in day money. Tuck grinned as she collected the envelope. It was exactly the amount she'd arrived with at her first rodeo.

As she started back toward home, Tuck saw Jona waiting for her. The parking area was alive with people-traffic, little kids darting around, reaching to pet the horses. Scat and Indigo walked slowly among them, their coats looking purplish in the blue-white arena lights. Tuck glanced at the narrow face under Jona's fancy feather-banded western hat. It looked friendly.

"Congratulations, Tuck. That little mare can really scoot. You fell into a pot of honey, getting her."

Tuck glowed, then remembered to be polite. "I'm sorry you were out of the money."

Jona shrugged. "It was my fault. I got careless with my legs. Listen, Tuck. . . ."

"Yeah?"

"You want a little advice? Of course, who am I to give you advice when you finished in the money and I was way out of the ballpark?" Jona grinned, and Tuck warmed to her like she'd never expected to.

"Heck, I need all the advice I can get. Shoot."

"You're leaning into the turns too much."

Tuck looked surprised. "I thought I had to."

"No. Your horse has to. What you have to do is stay as straight up and down as you can, even though your horse is laid out almost to the ground. See, when you lean in toward the barrel, your horse has to lean out just a hair of a shade in order to balance your weight over hers. Otherwise she could lose her balance and fall. I was watching your mare. She's got a lot of sense. She's watching those barrels and shortening her strides just right coming into them, and she's taking off from her hocks on the getaways. She's got all the talent she needs to be a top barrel horse. All she needs from you is for you not to interfere with her balance around the turns, and right now you're doing that by leaning too far in. Just hold yourself straight up and I'll bet you anything you'll shave your time."

"Thanks. I will." Tuck reined in and looked directly at Jona. "But how's come you're giving me advice, when I'm the competition?"

Jona grinned. " 'Cause I think Scat and I will beat you anyway, next time. And I want to win over topflight competitors."

B.C. refused to take Tuck's prize money when she tried to give it to him after the show that night. "No, now, you got more pressing uses for that money, hon. You lock it away and see if you can't build it into the five hundred you need to get your buckle back. If you can't, then you can pay me back with it. And if you can, then it's a sure bet you'll be able to pay me back at the next rodeo or the next."

The next morning the practice barrels were set up behind the arena for anyone who wanted to use them. The arena itself was being harrowed and sprinkled and groomed for the day's performance. Tuck was the first in line. She took Indigo through at a controlled pace, and when they came to the turn she concentrated on keeping her body straight up. Her foot touched the ground as Indigo dipped into the turn. It was a good turn, Tuck could feel that, but whether it was any better than they'd been doing, she couldn't tell. It occurred to her that Jona might be trying to sabotage her, but when she watched the other girls do their practice runs she could see they were all staying upright in the corners, too. She quit doubting Jona and went to cussing herself for not noticing something that obvious before.

"Ann Tucker on deck."

She was the fifth racer that night. Seventeen one twenty-six was the time to beat. Tuck nodded to the gate man and put Indigo in her warm-up spin. The mare was tight tonight, and so was Tuck.

"Hooeee!" she yelled into the black ears, and they were off. It was good. Indigo was on fire. Tuck was on fire. The barrel seemed to spin around them as Indigo and Tuck balanced through the turn. No time to think about it. Tuck's legs scissored around Indigo's barrel, swinging the horse while holding her straight, popping her into her lead change and feeling the leap, the power, the glory, amen. Second barrel, third barrel, perfect, then, "Hooeee!" the run, the last chance for every drop of speed Indigo had in her.

After the stop Tuck's whole body buzzed. Again there was applause, no more and no less than for the other good runs. Tuck felt light-headed.

Don't pass out now, you fool, she told herself. Not till you hear. . . .

"Time for Ann Tucker, sixteen and eight fifty-nine. That's the time to beat, and it's going to take a whale of a

146

run to do it, folks. That was one fine can-chase, ladies and gentlemen."

Sixteen and eight fifty-nine. The numbers passed like a glory banner through Tuck's head. She got off and burried her face against Indigo's neck, suddenly overcome by love and pride.

"That's the last time anybody calls you a dink, or me either," she whispered.

But Mason heard her. He'd come up close when she wasn't looking. He dropped an arm around her shoulder and gave it a squeeze. "Hey there, Tin Can Tucker," he grinned. "Good work."

Together they listened for the times of the remaining runs, but nobody came close to breaking seventeen. In the prize envelope that night was three hundred sixty dollars. First place day money.

She didn't wait around that night to watch Mason in team roping. Instead she socked away her money and took the slip of paper with Merrill's home phone number out of her gym bag and went to the arena office in search of a phone. Four hundred seventy-two dollars wasn't quite five, but close enough, she thought. Close enough to call and tell Merrill the money was coming.

He wasn't at home. She hadn't expected him to be. But his wife or whoever it was gave Tuck the number at the motel in Waco where Merrill was staying that week.

"Who is this?" the woman wanted to know.

"Ann Tucker. I'm a barrel racer. Mr. Merrill sold me a horse last spring and he was holding a trophy buckle for me till I could get the money to pay for her. You wouldn't happen to know if he's got the buckle with him, would you? I was calling to tell him I've got the money now, or at least I will by tomorrow or the next day."

There was a pause on the line. "Was that a sort of old-looking silver buckle with a ruby on it?"

"Yes! Do you have it there?"

"Oh, I'm sorry, hon. He sold that just last week."

"He *what*?" Tuck screeched.

"Well, if that's the buckle I'm thinking of, he did. But you better talk to him about it."

"Damn right I will." She hung up hard and called the motel in Waco. No answer in Merrill's room. Of course not, she told herself, not at nine o'clock. He'd still be at his rodeo.

She found Grace in the stands and slumped down beside her. "I just talked to Merrill's wife. She said he sold my buckle. Last week."

"He what?" Grace came as upright as her round little body could.

"Yeah. That's what I said. I'm trying to call him to find out for sure. Grace, how could he sell it? My six months wasn't up yet. How could he sell it when he knew how much it meant to me? It was the only thing I had of my parents, parent, whoever."

Grace reached high to get an arm around Tuck's shoulder. She patted and it helped, but it didn't make the sickness go away. Grace wouldn't leave the stands until after the bull riding, as though her presence would keep B.C. safe through it. But when it was over she took Tuck home to the Champion and gave her a beer. It tasted awful, but Tuck drank it in appreciation of the gesture

148

anyhow. Then, together, they went back to the telephone.

It was after eleven before Merrill finally answered.

"This is Ann Tucker," Tuck said in a hard voice. "You were supposed to hold my buckle for me for six months. I just talked to your wife and she said you sold it. Did you?"

She hoped. . . .

"Oh, I'm sorry, hon."

Hope withered.

"I never reckoned to hear from you again, and that's the Lord's truth. I knew you'd gone on home with the Olmsteads, and since I didn't hear a peep from you all this time, heck, I figured it was a lost cause. So I was keeping an eye on the price of silver, and it started going downhill last week, so I reckoned I'd best cash in on that buckle before it went any lower. By the way, I only got three hundred dollars for it, and the mare was priced at five, you remember—"

"You'll get your money." Tuck could hardly talk for clenching her teeth. "And by the way, in case you're interested, that mare you sold me just won top money tonight, barrel racing. I just thought you might like to know she didn't turn out to be such a dink after all. Now listen. We'll be here at the Billings rodeo for four more days. You send me written proof that all you got for that buckle was three hundred dollars, and I'll send you the other two hundred, and after that, that's it, buster."

She slammed the phone down and stalked away, furious, trying not to bawl, and blind to Grace trotting in her wake.

*   *   *

149

They sat outside far into the night, Tuck and Grace and B.C. and Mason and Jona, eating ice cream and drinking beer. Mason had made a run into town for cheer-up supplies when he heard the news. It was a crisp, cool night, full of brilliant stars now that the arena lights were off and the grounds darkened. Music came softly from a distant rig. Johnny Cash, walking the line. Indigo lay curled like a dog in her sleeping position by the trailer.

"I feel like I ran a race and fell off a cliff at the end of it," Tuck said.

Mason, who was sprawled on the ground near her chair, hit her booted toe with his fist. "Listen, Tucker. You won your race. You were shooting to get five hundred dollars before your deadline, and you did it, or you will have by tomorrow, at any rate. Just because Merrill finked out on you, that doesn't make it your failure."

She thought about it. "That's true."

"Well, if you ask me," said Jona, who had been filled in on the buckle and its importance, "you still came out ahead of the deal, Tuck. I mean, I know the buckle was special to you and all that, but still. Do you know what a top barrel horse is worth these days? Eight, ten thousand, easily. I've heard of them selling for twice that, and the good ones usually can't be bought for any amount of money."

"That's true," Tuck said again. The talk went on around her, but her mind caught on what Jona had said.

Her eyes rested on Indigo. Such a special horse, she thought. No, it wouldn't have been right to get something that special, that easy. Just hocking a belt buckle for a few

150

months, even if it was an awful special buckle, that wasn't enough of a price to pay, not for Indigo. Something you love that much ought to be paid for by something that really costs you. No. It's right this way. I hate like hell to lose that buckle, but look what I've got. The best horse in the world. Grace and B.C. Friends. Hell, even a name I earned. Tin Can Tucker, he called me.

She grinned.

B.C. noticed and said, "Well, folks, either we succeeded in cheering our girl up, or else we succeeded in getting her drunk."

Tuck laughed, and so did everyone else.

When she finally rolled into her shelf-bed in the front end of the Champion, Tuck called to Grace and B.C. beyond their curtain, "Hey, you know what I'm going to do with all this money I'm making, after I pay off what I owe you, and the trailer and Merrill? I think I'm going to buy me a real barrel racing saddle. With a pink seat. I saw one in a catalog. Won't that look like the cat's dinner? And some fancy new boots for me. And a hat with a feather band. We're going to be beautiful, Indigo and me."

"Shut up and go to sleep," Grace bellowed.

It was the morning after the final day of the Billings rodeo. The three of them had been up most of the night celebrating and had slept late. Now, driven by Grace's impatience, B.C. and Tuck struggled with the awning on the Champion's flank. It was supposed to roll up like a giant window shade, but it kept going off crooked and getting hung up on its own wrinkles. Once more Tuck and B.C.

unrolled their respective corners and began walking, carefully, carefully, toward the motor home, keeping the tension even along the twelve-foot length of the awning roller. It got crooked again and jammed.

Grace took over Tuck's corner. "Here. You two are about as handy as screen doors on a submarine. Let me do it."

Tuck grinned and stepped aside. It wasn't a new grin; it had been on there since last night.

Under Grace's authority, the awning rolled all the way up, first try. Its aluminum corner posts were snapped into their holders on the Champion's wall, all battened down and ready to travel. While Tuck untied Indigo and led the mare into the trailer, B.C. stowed the lawn chairs in their compartments beneath the motor home's belly.

Tuck slammed the trailer door, then reached over the top to pat Indigo's rump. "Just a short run this time, old darlin'. Just up to Great Falls. We'll be there by suppertime."

"Not at the rate you two are moving," Grace said. She frowned at Tuck, then reached out and flipped up Tuck's shirttail. "Tuck in your tails, kid. You earned that thing. Wear it so people can see it, why don't you?"

Tuck stretched up and hauled in her stomach as she jammed the shirttail home. She looked down at the belt buckle, and ran her fingertips over its bronzed surface. Champion barrel racer, Billings Rodeo, it said.

The past four nights Indigo had raced home first once more, and second the other three times, for a six-run total time of one hundred two point three-eighty seconds, forty-five thousandths of a second better than any other racer there. A thousand dollars and the trophy buckle for winning the championship, and more than fourteen hundred dollars in day money.

A van full of cowboys slowed as it coasted past. The one near the window called to her, "Hey, Tucker. I hear you did pretty good last night."

"Yeah. Made traveling money anyhow."

They waved. "See you in Great Falls."

"See you."

"Hey, rich lady," Grace bellowed, "you riding with us? Get your tail in here. We got some miles to make."

Tuck climbed into her seat at the front beside Grace. She kicked off her boots and propped her feet up on the dash.

"What makes you so cheerful this morning?" she asked, slapping Grace's knee.

"Just my natural high spirits and sunny nature, I reckon."

As they rolled out onto the highway Tuck said, "B.C.?"

"What?"

"Now that I'm your foster kid, and a champion barrel racer, and richer than Hogan's goat, are you going to tell me?"

"Tell you what, hon?"

"What the B.C. stands for, of course."

"Beaucephalus Charlton."

"Oh, come on, B.C. It does not."

Grace gave her an elbow in the ribs. "Honey, save

153

your breath to cool your soup. He ain't never going to tell you. Reach over there with your toe, will you, and turn on the radio. I feel like singing."

"Me, too," Tuck said.

The Champion rolled north across Montana, spilling music out the windows for the birds.

10830304

FIC   Hall, Lynn
HAL
        Tin can Tucker

DATE			